The Audacious Auditions of Jimmy Catesby

Victoria Connelly

To Sue
wishing you a very
Merry Christmas. Hope
you enjoy Jimmy's story.
Best wishes

Cuthland Press

Victoria Connelly
x

Cover design by J D Smith.

Published by Cuthland Press.

ISBN: 978-1-910522-09-7

To Allan with love

1. OVER THE WALL

Jimmy Catesby's heart was hammering as if it meant to leap right out of his chest at any moment, and still he kept on running. He wasn't even sure where he was going. All he knew was that he had to keep on moving.

'Oi! Catesby!'

Jimmy glanced quickly over his shoulder. They were gaining on him. He had to run faster.

Turning the corner of Main Street, he took the muddy lane by the side of the church. For one second, his foot skidded. It had been raining the night before and running was difficult, but he couldn't afford to fall. Not here. Not yet.

The track went down to the fields where a public footpath led towards the woods. He hoped he would be safe there. He knew the woods better than anyone. But the woods were a long way off and he didn't know if he could make it.

It was then that he noticed the wall which surrounded Penham Manor. It was an old red brick wall which had mellowed and crumbled with time but, at eight feet high, it was still pretty unscalable. Unless …

Jimmy ran to the gate at the end of the track and climbed over it in one swift movement and then ran round the wall to the section which backed onto the fields. There were several trees there. If he could just find one that looked a little bit helpful.

This one. He stopped and looked up at the branches. They looked sturdy enough.

'Cates*by!*' a voice yelled from the lane. 'There's no

point running.'

He'd have to be quick. As soon as they were over the gate, they'd be able to see him.

Grabbing hold of a branch with both hands, he hoisted himself up and clambered into the heart of the tree. It was a good job he had a head for heights because he was soon dizzyingly high and could see over the wall into the grounds of Penham Manor. He gave a long, silent whistle at what greeted him. It was bigger than the school playing fields and it was beautiful. At the end closest to him was an apple orchard and the trees were still in blossom. The grass was long and unkempt but, towards the house, the garden was filled with enormous flower beds. There was even a small fountain and a garden swing.

Without further delay, Jimmy clambered across and swung himself out of the tree until he was sitting astride the wall. The only problem now was getting down. It was a lot higher than he'd first thought.

The sound of the two boys climbing over the gate at the end of the lane made him bold and he jumped, his body suspended in the air for one terrifying moment before he thudded to the ground.

He was still in one piece, he thought, pressing himself flat against the wall in case his pursuers thought to climb the tree and look over into the garden. As his heart continued to thud in his ears, he heard voices coming from the other side of the wall.

'Where did he go?'

'What're you asking me for? I don't know.'

'You said he went this way.'

'It was a guess.'

Jimmy heard one of the boys thump the other and a fight began. There was no mistaking who they were:

Dean Stoner and Jordan Wicks – the two most notorious boys in Penham. If a wall had been graffitied, it would be Stoner and Wicks. If a window had been broken, it would be Stoner and Wicks. If anything from anywhere had been stolen, smashed or wrecked, everyone would know who to blame. Stoner and Wicks were a two-man team from hell, sent to try the patience of the residents of Penham.

They were in year ten now and were known by their surnames because the bellowing sound of 'STONER!' and 'WICKS!' regularly echoed along the corridors of the school. The head of year ten, a rather old-fashioned man who wore faded tweed suits and had a beard you could lose a school dinner in, never called them by their Christian names. A deeply unlikeable pair, Dean Stoner was tall with gangly limbs which belied their strength. His face was long and thin too, and his eyes were permanently narrowed into a scowl. His school blazer was ripped in at least five places and he never wore a tie which earned him endless detentions. Jordan Wicks was stockier than Dean. His favourite pastime of bullying year sevens into emptying the edible contents of their pockets had meant his waist had expanded somewhat over the years. His face was, perhaps, the ugliest Jimmy had ever seen. He had tiny beady eyes and skin like a lumpy potato. His nose was large and crooked as if it had been broken which wouldn't come as a surprise as he was always getting himself into fights. No, Stoner and Wicks were the stuff of nightmares. They were the reason year six pupils dreaded going to Penham High School, and Jimmy was their current number one victim and he knew exactly why.

He kicked the ground in front of him. What was

their problem, anyway? Just because Jimmy wanted to be an actor and they had no idea about what they wanted to do with their future, it didn't mean that they had to have a go at him. For a moment, Jimmy allowed himself a little daydream about what would happen to Stoner and Wicks in the future. They'd probably be in prison before they were twenty. Jimmy smiled at the thought. And perhaps he would be acting with one of those drama companies that toured prisons, and perform in front of them. They'd see, then, how good he was. But the best thing about it would be that he would be able to get up and go home at the end of the performance whereas Stoner and Wicks would have to return to their grim cells which smelled like a public toilet and had bars across the windows.

'Leave it out, you maniac.'

The voice of Wicks broke into Jimmy's thoughts.

'You big baby,' Stoner laughed. 'Did I hurt you?'

Jimmy heard Wicks thumping Stoner.

'Hey!'

'What?'

'I thought we were meant to be after Catesby,' Wicks pointed out.

'Find him and he's mine,' Stoner said.

'He must've gone over the fields.'

'Where? He's not there. Look! We would've seen him.'

'The wall?'

'Don't be stupid. That's the old hag's place. Nobody goes in there,' Stoner said. 'Not unless they want to be boiled up and eaten.'

'That's gross!'

'It's the truth. She eats flesh. That's what I've

heard.'

Jimmy listened to them from the other side of the wall. His heart was racing again and his breathing was thick and fast, but they wouldn't be able to hear him – he felt quite confident about that. He just had to stay calm until they went away. He was quite an expert at getting himself out of scrapes now. He hadn't had much of a choice since they'd started picking on him. He could remember the exact moment it had all started. Jimmy had never been the sort to be bullied. He had always been popular at school. Until he'd started acting.

He still remembered the day he'd been on his way from double maths to history. The poster – an A3 job in red writing – had cried out for his attention.

Scenes from Shakespeare

Have you got what it takes to be an actor?
Find out at lunch time on Thursday in the drama studio.

Only eight pupils had turned up. *Eight* – out of the whole school. Jimmy had felt so embarrassed on behalf of Miss Parnaby, the drama teacher. She wasn't a full-time member of staff which Jimmy thought a great shame. Not that he fancied her or anything. Well, not much. But she was filled with an enthusiasm which was highly contagious and it annoyed him that so few pupils supported her.

She hadn't shown her disappointment, though. She'd simply beamed at those present and handed out some scripts.

'The thing to remember with Shakespeare is that his plays were written over four hundred years ago. That means that the language is very different from our own today, but his characters are just like you and me. They think about falling in love. They worry about pleasing their friends. They want to be the best.'

Jimmy had sat, spellbound. He wanted to be an actor. It was as simple as that. His whole life had become clear to him that day in the rather shabby drama studio. For years, he'd thought he'd probably just end up with a boring office job like his mum, but now he could see an alternative. A life on the stage. A life as an actor.

When he thought about it, he realised that he'd always loved acting. For as long as he could remember, he'd been an avid film fan, watching his favourite movies over and over again until he knew the lines not just of the hero and heroine, but all the other parts too. His mother thought he was crazy.

'Who is it today, Jimmy? Cary Grant or Tom Hanks?'

Yes, he could do a mean impersonation. Sometimes, it would make his mother laugh but, at other times, she'd yell at him.

'Have you nothing better to do than mess about playing pretend?'

He couldn't understand her change of attitude.

It had all began with a weekend of James Cagney films. As far as he was aware, he was the only boy in his school to have ever watched a black and white film.

'Mum?' he'd asked after doing nothing else but watching films that weekend.

'What?'

'Did you name me after James Cagney?' he asked hopefully.

'James Cagney?'

'The actor. You know – from *Public Enemy* and-'

'I know who he is. No!'

'Oh,' Jimmy said, feeling a little deflated.

But then she leaned forward and whispered in his ear. 'I named you after James Stewart.' And she kissed him on the cheek.

Jimmy beamed. James Stewart. He was an actor, wasn't he?

Shortly after that, Jimmy began his James Stewart faze watching and rewatching *The Philadelphia Story*, *Rear Window*, *It's a Wonderful Life* and *Destry Rides Again* until his mum banned them.

'Don't you know those movies inside out by now?'

'Yes,' Jimmy explained. Didn't she understand that *that* was where the pleasure lay? A good film was like a good meal: it was a pleasure so wonderful that the experience was only enriched by repetition. But he'd never actually thought that he could become an actor himself. Until he'd seen Miss Parnaby's poster.

Now, with his back pressed up against the wall of Penham Manor, he realised he might have made the biggest mistake of his life because *Scenes from Shakespeare* had involved wearing tights, and a year 7 boy in tights wasn't normal, was it? You were asking for trouble if you started dressing up in tights and pantaloons, and it was generally agreed that you deserved all the trouble you got.

'I'm not hangin' round here all day,' Stoner suddenly said, spitting loudly onto the ground.

'Come on, then. Let's go to the allotments. Old man Fraser's been plantin' again.'

'What? Is he stupid?'

Stoner and Wicks laughed and, to Jimmy's intense

relief, ran off.

For a few minutes, Jimmy didn't dare move. He stood as still as a garden statue, letting his breathing slow down, but he couldn't stay there forever. His mum would be home from work now and would be wondering where he was. He prised himself away from the wall, wondering how he was going to get out of the garden. There weren't any trees to climb on this side of the wall so he couldn't go back the way he'd come. He looked around the garden for some sort of exit, but the wall appeared to go all the way round. He'd have to try his luck nearer the house. Surely, there'd be some way out round the side.

He made his way through the orchard, white blossom flurrying over him in a little snowstorm. The orchard led into the more formal garden that Jimmy had spied from the tree, and he stood for a moment by an ornamental pond, smiling at the enormous orange fish that were swimming like submarines in the dark water.

He could have stayed there all day, but he suddenly realised that he wasn't alone and, spinning round, he came face to face with an old woman.

'Who are you?' she said. 'And what are you doing in my garden?'

2. MISS MARY SNOW

Jimmy found himself staring at a woman with a perfect halo of white hair. He had never seen hair that white before. Old people's hair was usually grey or, at best, the white of snow after a couple of days of being trudged in. But her hair positively glowed.

'What are you doing here?' she asked again, her face concerned rather than cross, much to Jimmy's relief.

'I was just-' What was he meant to say? He didn't want to own up to being chased by Stoner and Wicks. How would that make him look?

'Having a look round my garden?'

Jimmy's mouth dropped open. 'No – I – well … '

'It is rather beautiful, isn't it?'

'Y-yes.'

She sighed, obviously deciding not to question him further on how he came to be standing by her ornamental pond. 'As long as you haven't come to rob me. You haven't come to rob me, have you? Or throw eggs at my windows? Or graffiti anything?'

'NO!' Jimmy said, aghast.

'Very glad to hear it.' She turned away from him and walked towards the house.

Jimmy watched, not quite knowing what to do.

'Well, come on then,' she said, not bothering to look back.

Once inside the house, Jimmy's mouth dropped open in surprise. He'd never known his grandparents but, from what he'd seen on television shows, this didn't look much like an old lady's home. He'd expected something more gloomy – maybe a few rather dark pieces of furniture, and sofas with a heavy pattern, and those lacy things on the backs of chairs and little spindly side tables. Old people didn't do modern, it was a known fact and yet this room was light, bright and beautiful. The furniture was sleek and pale and there was absolutely nothing about it that smelt like a musty old library.

'You look hungry,' she said. 'Are you hungry?'

'I'm not sure,' he said, the question taking him completely by surprise.

'Not sure if you're hungry or not?' she asked, her pale grey eyes widening in surprise. 'Well, I was just about to have some tea and biscuits. Would you like some? Have a seat.' And she left the room. He was a complete stranger whom she'd found in her garden and yet she'd invited him into her home for tea and biscuits. Was she completely mad?

Yes!

That was the only answer. She must be a complete loony and wasn't going for tea and biscuits at all. It was just a ploy. She was in the kitchen sharpening her knife. Stoner and Wicks had been right. He was going to be murdered. Murdered by a little old lady. Boiled and eaten!

Jimmy felt the palms of his hands becoming sticky with sweat. He had to get out of there. He nervously looked for the fastest exit and was just about to leg it out of the living room when the old lady appeared.

'Oh, are you leaving already?'

Jimmy stopped dead in his tracks. 'Got to get home. Mum's expecting me.'

'So soon? But your tea-' she said, and her face was at once warm and gentle. Had he misjudged her? 'Why not have a little something before you go?'

Jimmy looked at her. She didn't look much like a flesh-eating granny. She looked like a sweet old lady to him, and he *was* feeling rather hungry.

'Go on,' she said, obviously seeing him eyeing up the plate of biscuits she was carrying. 'Sit down and have some of these.'

Jimmy did as he was told, reaching out to take a ginger biscuit and biting into it.

'Good?'

He nodded his appreciation.

'I made them.'

Jimmy swallowed anxiously. They were probably poisoned. He wasn't sure how you could tell – until it was too late.

'Anything the matter?' the old lady asked.

Jimmy shook his head.

The old lady suddenly clapped her hands. 'How very rude of me. You have no idea who I am, do you? And I've no idea who you are. Well,' she smiled, 'we can soon put that right, can't we? I'm Mary Snow.'

Jimmy wiped his mouth free from ginger biscuit crumbs. 'Jimmy,' he said. 'Jimmy Catesby.'

'Nice to meet you, Jimmy Catesby,' Miss Snow said, leaning forward from her chair to shake his hand. Her hand was warm and papery and she wore an enormous amethyst ring which glowed in the light of the room. 'And where do you live?'

'Here in Penham,' he said. 'The other end – one of the new houses.'

Miss Snow nodded. 'So what brings you here?'

Jimmy pursed his lips together. There was no getting away from it this time. 'I got lost,' he said. 'Thought this was a short cut back to the main road.'

'Oh,' Miss Snow said, nodding. 'Now, why don't

you tell me the truth?'

'That *is* the truth.'

Miss Snow shook her head. 'Almost convincing. You'd be a good actor, though' she said. 'With a bit of training of course.'

Jimmy's eyebrows rose. Was she being serious? Did she really think he could be an actor? Should he tell her that that was exactly what he wanted to be? She didn't look like the sort of grown-up who'd tell him not to be so silly and that he'd be better off studying law or medicine.

'Miss – er – Snow,' he began.

She smiled warmly. 'Yes?'

'I want to-' he stopped.

'What?' she asked.

'I think I want…'

She frowned as if trying to understand. 'The toilet? You want the toilet?' she asked. 'Oh, how silly of me. You should have said. It's through there on the left.'

'No,' he said, blushing furiously. 'I want to be an actor. I mean, when I grow up.'

Miss Snow looked at him, her pretty grey eyes glittering. 'Why wait until you grow up?'

'Pardon?' It wasn't quite the response he'd expected.

'I said, why wait? There are so many wonderful roles for youngsters – I mean – boys. Not just in films but on stage too. Have you thought about the stage?'

Jimmy nodded. He thought of little else. Whole lessons would fly by at school and he wouldn't have taken in a single word because, in his imagination, he was on the stage, acting out some scene or other he'd been reading the night before, planning out his movements, his gestures, his entrances and exits. And the applause. He liked that part the most. The curtain call. Sometimes in his imagination, his curtain calls would be longer than the actual plays themselves.

'Never forget the stage,' Miss Snow said. 'It's an actor's best friend and wisest teacher.'

Jimmy was very excited by this. Nobody had ever talked to him this way before. 'Do you really think I could be one?'

Miss Snow looked at him closely for a moment. 'Yes,' she said. 'I do, but you have a lot to learn.'

Jimmy leant forward. 'Like what?'

'Did you notice what you were doing when you were telling me that lie?'

'No.'

'You were spinning your biscuit on the plate. Round and round it was going. Did you not realise?'

'No,' Jimmy said, utterly aghast at having betrayed himself.

'A sure sign of nerves. A lot of people do that when they're nervous. Not spinning biscuits – I mean, fiddling. Women fiddle with jewellery – they twist rings and bracelets and things. A man might develop a sudden scratching behind his ear or fiddle with a pair of glasses.'

'One of our teachers does that at school.'

'There, you see.'

'Does that mean he's nervous?'

'Sometimes. It could just be he's done it for so many years that it's become a habit.'

'How do you know all this?'

Miss Snow smiled. 'Because I was an actress.'

Jimmy's eyes almost popped out of his head. 'An *actress*?'

Miss Snow laughed. 'Don't look so surprised. I

haven't been an old lady all my life, you know.'

'Oh, I didn't mean-'

Miss Snow laughed again at his embarrassment. 'Come and see this,' she said, getting up and walking over to one of the sleek side tables where she picked up a silver frame and held it out for Jimmy to inspect. It was a photograph of a beautiful young woman with long golden hair adorned with flowers. She was wearing a long pale dress and had a faraway expression in her eyes.

'1947,' she said.

Jimmy gave a long low whistle. It was a date from a history book to him it seemed so long ago.

'Ophelia,' she said.

'From *Hamlet*?'

Miss Snow looked pleasantly surprised. 'Yes,' she said. 'You really *do* want to be an actor, don't you?'

Jimmy nodded.

'Well, you've come to the right place.'

3. ACTING, NOT LYING

Jimmy put his key in the lock and opened the front door as quietly as possible, sneaking through the hallway and up the stairs.

'Is that you, Jimmy?'

Drat! His mum had heard him. He'd been hoping he could get to his room and pretend he'd been there for ages.

'Yes, Mum,' he called and his mother appeared in the hallway, a dark scowl on her face.

'Where've you been? I've been worried sick!'

'Nowhere.'

'Don't tell me *nowhere*. It's nearly six o'clock, Jimmy. Where've you been all this time, eh?'

'Just round the shops. I told you I was going after school.'

'Did you?' His mother frowned again.

'You're getting so forgetful, Mum,' he said. He was a good actor when he needed to be and it got him out of all sorts of scrapes.

'What have you got to go shopping for? I don't suppose you bought anything useful like a loaf of bread. I can't believe the amount of bread you get through. You'll end up looking like a slice of toast if you carry on.'

'I went to the bookshop.'

'Bookshop? What were you doing there?'

Jimmy sighed. He'd have thought his mum would be happy about his interest in books, but she wasn't; she was suspicious. What young lad wanted to buy books with his pocket money? It wasn't normal.

'Shouldn't you be into cartoons or football

magazines?' she asked, thoroughly bemused by her son.

'I like books, Mum,' he tried to explain – again. 'Plays. I like reading plays.'

'Can't you borrow them from the library?'

'Have you been in the library? There are more computers than books now and they never have any plays, or else I've read all the ones they've got.'

'Oh,' his mum said.

'I'd like my own copies anyway,' he explained, thinking of his growing collection of which he was so proud. 'They're not cheap, but they're cheaper than smoking.'

'What did you say?'

'I said, it's cheaper than smoking.'

'Are you having a go at me for smoking, cause if you are, James Catesby, you'd better think again. Smoking's all I've got so don't you dare criticise me for it.'

'I wasn't, Mum.'

'Well, it sounded like you were.'

'I was just saying that I don't smoke.'

'Of course you don't smoke. You're twelve years old.'

Jimmy shook his head and didn't bother to explain that plenty of the kids in his year smoked. They'd spend pounds and pounds without their parents noticing.

He wished his mother didn't smoke. The house stank and there was a permanent fog in the kitchen even though she assured him she never smoked more than ten a day. Whenever she went out, he'd open all the windows in an attempt to air the place and his mother bought nasty air fresheners and plug-ins that invaded his nostrils and were more offensive than the smoke itself.

Anyway, his mother wasn't looking convinced by Jimmy's latest trip to the bookshop.

'What did you buy, then? Let's see.'

Jimmy opened up his rucksack and rummaged around, producing a book.

'*The Whistler*? What's that?'

'It's a play. By Corin Maxwell,' he said, handing it to her.

'I can see that. It's not in very good condition, is it?' she said, flicking through the pages. 'Someone's scribbled in it.'

'It's second-hand. They sell second-hand books there now.'

'Do they? I didn't know that.'

He nodded. They didn't, of course. He was lying. Well, not lying exactly – *stretching the truth. Acting!* They *could* sell second-hand books, couldn't they? It wasn't completely unheard of. No, Jimmy didn't like the word *lying*. It implied he was deceitful and he wasn't. He was only acting and that couldn't be wrong, could it? People made careers of it. *He* wanted to make a career out of it so, to his mind, he had to practise.

'It's not a very big section,' he continued, getting into the spirit of his second-hand book story, 'but they've got some interesting plays and things. I'll have to go again sometime soon.' There, he thought. That should cover him for another visit to Miss Snow's.

His mother handed the book back and Jimmy placed it carefully in his bag. It had been lent to him by Miss Snow.

'This was one of my first plays,' she'd told him. 'I think you'll like it. I played Irene – the daughter. I can imagine you as Stephen.'

Jimmy hadn't been able to wait until he'd got home. He'd flicked through the play as he'd jogged, but it was impossible to read on the move so he'd hidden the book in his bag to save for later.

Now, sitting in his room, he read and read until his eyes were red. Two hours later, and he'd finished the play. Miss Snow had been right. He *could* play Stephen – the misunderstood son bullied by his father and ignored by his mother. He flicked through the Stephen scenes again, committing line after line to memory.

When his mother knocked on his door, he got the shock of his life. That's what happened when he started to read: he was no longer a part of the real world – he would take off and be living in another reality.

He got up off his bed and unlocked the door.

'Jimmy! What have I told you about locking your door? What reason have you got to lock yourself in here?' she said, barging in.

'Mum!'

'Well, really, Jimmy.' She looked round his bedroom, her eyes narrowed in suspicion as if there really might be a girl hiding behind his curtains or tucked under the bedding. 'What have you been doing up here all this time? Homework?'

Jimmy nodded, quietly cursing to himself that he'd completely forgotten about his English and geography homework.

'What's wrong with you – your eyes are all screwed up?'

'Just tired, Mum.'

'You sure you don't need glasses?'

Jimmy sighed. How many times had she asked him that? 'I don't need glasses, Mum. My eyes are fine.'

She peered closely at him and then licked her fingers and stroked his hair back.

'Aw, *Mum!*'

'That's better,' she said.

'I'm going to bed. What does it matter what my hair looks like?'

'You should always take a pride in how you look,' she said, self-consciously fiddling with her own hair even though there was nobody but Jimmy to see it.

'You look fine, Mum.' He smiled. He'd inherited his mother's dark curly hair and bright blue eyes. He even had the same spattering of freckles over his nose.

She leant forward to kiss him. 'Wash and brush and straight to bed,' she said. She'd been telling him the same thing for as long as he could remember. He'd be an old man and she'd still be telling him the same thing. He could imagine himself in an old person's home. The matron would come in and tell him he'd had a phone call from his mother.

'She said-'

'Wash and brush and straight to bed,' Jimmy would interrupt, shuffling along to the bathroom in an ancient dressing gown and a pair of slippers that had seen better days.

'Night, Jimmy,' his mum said now.

'Night, Mum.'

As soon as he was washed and dressed for bed, Jimmy got his school books out.

Write about a time when you felt lonely, his English assignment read. For a moment, he imagined Miss Snow in her huge manor house on her own. Was she lonely? She'd seemed happy enough, but she'd looked so disappointed when he'd said he had to leave even though he'd promised call again.

It was half-past eleven by the time he got to his geography: three boring questions about the Industrial Revolution. If he was an insomniac, it would have been a miracle cure.

Climbing into bed a quarter of an hour later, he gazed at the movie posters that surrounded him. *North by Northwest. Angels with Dirty Faces. Forrest Gump.* He tried to imagine his freckly face on a poster. Could he really become an actor? Was he the stuff that movies were made of?

He thought of Miss Snow again. She'd been so encouraging. He'd never known anyone like her before. They'd talked and talked as if they'd known each other all their lives. He wondered why he'd never known that she lived there. How had he overlooked a famous actress on his very own doorstep?

Jimmy closed his eyes with a big smile on his face. He would dream of being a famous stage actor, of being discovered by Hollywood, of …

But he didn't. Dreams – or rather nightmares – didn't work like that. They had little regard for what you wanted. They sneaked up on you, wrapping their terrifying tentacles around your imagination, suffocating you with horror.

Jimmy was running. The lane was never-ending and they were catching up with him. He had to get to the gate, but it kept getting further and further away. He looked up at the wall but it seemed to reach into the very heavens. There was no escape.

'CATESBY!'

Two pairs of hands grabbed him and flung him to the ground before picking him up again and slamming him against the wall. He didn't see their faces, but he didn't need to. He knew who they were.

When he woke up the next morning, he felt more exhausted than when he'd gone to bed and his eyes were still red raw.

4. PUTTING YOURSELF OUT THERE

Mr Fortescue stood at the front of the class, glaring at 7B, his dark eyebrows hanging thickly over his eyes like a pair of squirrel tails.

'I'm waiting,' he said in a dangerously quiet monotone.

An instant hush fell as thirty bottoms stopped shuffling in their chairs and thirty pairs of eyes focussed on the teacher.

'You've already added three minutes' detention to the end of this lesson,' he said, his beady eyes scanning the room.

Jimmy sighed inwardly. It was the last lesson of the day and Mr Fortescue was not a reasonable man and hardly a lesson went by when they weren't kept in for some unpardonable sin or other. Jimmy thought Fortescue must surely have been a sergeant major in a previous lifetime. He had that look about him. His back was always ramrod straight and he had the most unnerving stare as if he could see all the rebellious thoughts of pupils whirring away inside their brains.

Finally, once he was completely convinced that nobody was talking, moving or breathing, he began.

'Turn to page seventy-two.'

Everybody did as they were told.

'Read the double page and do questions one to five.'

And that was it. That was his total participation as a teacher. He didn't even bother to introduce the subject, but Jimmy saw that it was the English Civil War. It had been the same routine all year. Mr

Fortescue had never actually taught them. 7B and, Jimmy assumed, every other class he taught, had been given a book to work through by themselves. It was outrageous. If Jimmy hadn't been so scared of old Fortescue he would have reported him. Instead, he just got on with it, like everybody else, whilst Fortescue sat at his desk reading a John Grisham novel.

Jimmy glanced round the classroom. He hated being treated like this. It wasn't fair, but he knew there was nothing he could do about it and that made him even more angry. He looked at the other pupils. Matthew Bradstock, 7B's genius, had already power-read the set pages and was speed writing with his expensive fountain pen. He would, no doubt, be given some extension work to do: an ancient photocopied worksheet which Fortescue kept in one of his desk drawers. Jimmy suspected that they never got marked. Their books hadn't been marked since Christmas and Fortescue never even bothered to walk around the classroom to make sure pupils were actually doing the work set.

Sighing deeply – and silently – Jimmy began reading about roundheads and cavaliers.

It was about twenty minutes later when he got into trouble. They were sitting in alphabetical order which meant that Jimmy was next to Freddie Chapman, who hardly ever spoke because of a rather pronounced stutter. He was also painfully shy and wouldn't have dared to put his hand up even if his pants were on fire.

'J-Jimmy?' Freddie whispered.

Jimmy glanced at Freddie in silent response.

'I'm stuck on question two.'

Jimmy, who was on question four, slowly pushed his exercise book towards Freddie for him to copy. There was no way he was going to explain the answer to him. That would have been too risky.

'Hurry up,' he whispered, watching as Freddie copied the answer in his painfully slow handwriting.

'CATESBY!'

Jimmy jolted to attention.

'What are you doing, boy?'

Jimmy desperately wanted to reply, 'Helping Freddie because you haven't explained the work properly like a half-decent teacher would. And don't call me 'Catesby' or 'boy'. It's extremely rude and my name is Jimmy. Or James, if you must.'

However, Jimmy replied, 'Nothing, sir.'

Fortescue scraped his chair back and stood up. It was about as active as he got. 'Come here, Catesby.'

Jimmy sighed and got up, walking to the front of the classroom, twenty-nine pairs of eyes following his progress and thanking their lucky stars that it wasn't them.

Reaching Fortescue's desk, Jimmy looked him in the eye.

'I will NOT have pupils cheating in my class.'

'I wasn't cheating, sir.'

Fortescue's face looked as if it were about to explode. One of his eyes had narrowed into an ugly squint and his eyebrows were twitching in a hairy dance.

'DON'T answer me back, boy!'

Jimmy could feel his eyeballs vibrating at Fortescue's words as his face was showered in vitriolic spit. He sincerely believed that, had corporal punishment been allowed, the palm of his hand and his rump would have been laced with angry cane marks by now. Instead, Fortescue pointed a furious finger towards the door.

'OUT!' he barked. 'I don't want to see you until the end of the lesson. You will stay behind and finish your work then.'

Jimmy opened his mouth to protest but, as he saw Fortescue was about to burst a blood vessel, he shut it again and left the classroom in silence, standing in the draughty corridor for the remainder of the lesson.

He was furious. He was going to be late now. He'd planned on going to see Miss Snow after school and every minute was precious. His mum would become suspicious if he was any later home than last time so Jimmy had planned on running to Penham Manor straight after school.

He stared into the classroom through the window in the door. His mother had told him you shouldn't hate people but, at that moment, he couldn't help hating Mr Fortescue. He was going to ruin everything.

He wondered if the film star Cary Grant had had to put up with such appalling teachers at school.

It seemed an age until the end of the lesson and 7B filed out to go home. Fortescue beckoned Jimmy back into the classroom with a solitary movement of his finger. He wasn't even going to waste his breath on Jimmy.

Jimmy got his books and bag and moved to the front of the class. He knew the routine having helped Freddie out with his answers in the past and being caught. Fortescue sat down at his desk and stuck his nose into his paperback. His addiction to bestselling fiction was the only indication that he was human.

For a brief moment, Jimmy wondered if he should strike up a conversation and imagined how the scene might go.

'Excuse me, sir. Is your novel good?'

Fortescue would look up, surprised and yet delighted. 'As a matter of fact, it is. You should read it.'

'Do you think so, sir? I like thrillers.'

'I'll lend it to you,' he'd say, a rare smile crossing his face. 'Tell you what – why don't you run along home and take this book with you. Let me know what you think of it.'

'Okay, sir. Thanks, sir.'

Jimmy shook his head and rolled his eyes. Looking at Fortescue's stony face, that scenario wasn't very likely, was it?

Jimmy ploughed on through the final question and then raised his hand. Fortescue pretended not to notice until Jimmy had to cradle his arm with the other and clear his throat.

'You finished, Catesby?'

'Yes, sir.'

Fortescue gave a cursory glance over Jimmy's book, but didn't bother reading it. 'I won't have you swapping answers in my class, is that understood?' His dark brows hovered menacingly over his eyes.

'Yes, sir,' Jimmy said when what he really wanted to do was to tie those rotten eyebrows into a knot and punch him on the nose.

'Right, put your chair up and be off with you.'

Jimmy did as he was told and ran out of school as fast as his legs would carry him.

Penham High was a good half mile away from what was now referred to as 'Old Penham' – the winding main road lined with pretty, red-bricked cottages. It was also the opposite direction from where Jimmy's house was, but he'd told Miss Snow that he'd visit her after school and he was desperate to talk to her about the play he'd read.

Turning the corner, Jimmy could see Penham Manor and the church. Unfortunately, he could also see Stoner and Wicks. And Freddie Chapman.

Stoner was pushing Freddie around whilst Wicks was hovering menacingly in the background. Jimmy could feel his blood boiling. Freddie was an easy target with his shyness and his stutter and it made Jimmy so angry that Stoner and Wicks picked on such victims.

He could feel his heart hammering inside his chest because he knew he couldn't just turn around and pretend he'd seen nothing. There were plenty of people who could have done just that, but Jimmy wasn't one of them. For a moment, he wondered what to do. Him and Freddie against Stoner and Wicks was a non-starter. He turned around as if there might be some help at hand, but what was he expecting to see? A policeman walking down the road with a Stoner-sized truncheon? No such luck. He was on his own with only his wits to keep him company.

Swallowing hard, Jimmy yelled at the top of his voice, 'OI, STONER!'

Stoner and Wicks turned so fast it was a wonder their necks didn't break. Jimmy waited an anxious few seconds before he was sure he had their attention and then he ran. He couldn't take the path down the side of the church and jump into Penham Manor over the wall as he had done before because Stoner and Wicks were blocking it, so he ran back towards the centre of the village. There was an alleyway which would take him to the fields and he could get round to Miss Snow's from there. He had a good head start so he should be able to make it without being seen.

His boots thudded down the road as he ran. He was a good runner. He'd always preferred athletics to games at school and it was standing him in good stead now. Until he reached the alleyway.

Stoner and Wicks were gaining on him. He looked over his shoulder. They saw him duck down the alley and were fast on his trail. He wasn't going to make it. He-

A pair of strong hands grabbed his shoulders and he hit the ground before he knew what was happening.

It was just like in his dream only he knew he wasn't going to wake up from this one.

'Look what we've got here,' Stoner said, his knee hard in the centre of Jimmy's chest and his ugly face hovering over him.

Wicks spat on the ground. He was bright red from the exertion of running.

'Tights Boy Catesby!' Wicks sneered.

'Yeah. Where are your tights now?' Stoner said, pulling up one of the legs of Jimmy's trousers. 'He hasn't got them on!'

'Get his trousers off,' Wicks said.

Stoner scowled and then laughed like a mad hyena and started tugging at Jimmy's belt. Jimmy struggled but Stoner was at least twice as strong as him.

'He's a skinny little Tights Boy,' Stoner said through gritted teeth as he continued to pull at the belt.

'He's ugly too,' Wicks joined.

Jimmy couldn't believe what he was hearing. Had Wicks not looked in a mirror recently?

'Maybe he only wears tights in the privacy of his bedroom. And make-up too, eh, Tights Boy? Some nice eye-shadow and lipstick? Does your mum know you steal her make-up?'

'Shut up!' Jimmy dared to yell.

Stoner slapped him hard across the face. 'Don't you tell me to shut up!'

'Someone's coming,' Wicks suddenly said.

Stoner grunted in annoyance, but at least he'd stopped pulling. 'You haven't heard the last of this, Catesby!' he spat, ripping Jimmy's rucksack off his back, opening it up and spilling the contents onto the muddy track. Jimmy tried not to yell out loud as he saw Miss Snow's copy of *The Whistler* falling into a puddle.

'Come ON!' Wicks said in warning.

Stoner gave Jimmy's leg a parting kick before the two of them ran off down the alley.

When he was quite sure they'd gone, Jimmy sat up, quickly doing his belt up and brushing his coat down. He was a mess. What was worse, though, was that the entire contents of his bag were wet and covered in mud. How could he go to Miss Snow's now? How was he going to explain?

He picked up *The Whistler*. It was soaked through and streaked with dirt. He put it in his bag and collected his school books and packed lunch box. Everything was filthy, but he wasn't going to let Stoner and Wicks get the better of him. They weren't going to stop him from visiting Miss Snow.

Swinging his rucksack onto his back, Jimmy walked out of the alleyway onto the main road.

Freddie had long gone – obviously having made the most of his chance of escape when Jimmy had intervened. Now, the coast was clear and he headed to Miss Snow's.

Penham Manor was easily the largest house in the village with beautiful curving Dutch gables and large sash windows. The front, which looked out onto the road, was smothered with pale purple wisteria.

Jimmy went up to the impressive white front door and knocked. He still wasn't sure what he was going to say.

Miss Snow answered with a bright smile, but it soon faded when she saw the state of Jimmy.

'What on earth happened to you?' she asked, her face creased with concern.

'I fell over,' Jimmy said lamely.

Miss Snow stared at him and he knew she didn't believe him.

Ushering him inside, she tried again. 'Looks like you were pushed to me.'

Jimmy took his bag and coat off and Miss Snow motioned for him to sit down. He looked up at her and swallowed.

'I'm a bit dirty,' he said.

Miss Snow nodded and grabbed a blanket from one of her chairs.

'Sit on that,' she said. 'Now, who did this to you?'

'Two boys from school.'

'Older boys?'

'Yes,' Jimmy said.

Miss Snow sat down opposite him. 'These wouldn't be the same two boys who were seen running away from the allotments last week having completely ruined Albert Fraser's patch?'

'Probably,' Jimmy said, remembering their dialogue from the other side of the wall when he'd first climbed over into Penham Manor to escape from them.

'They have to be stopped,' Miss Snow said, shaking her head. 'Does your mother know about them?'

Jimmy bit his lip. 'I don't like to bother her about them.'

Miss Snow frowned. 'But mothers are there to be bothered.'

'She'd just make things worse. She'd want to go to school and have them expelled and they'd take it out on me in the end.'

'But they shouldn't be allowed to get away with it. Is it only you they pick on?'

Jimmy shook his head. 'They were picking on Freddie, but I got their attention to help him out.'

'Oh!' Miss Snow's hands flew to her face. 'You dear boy. And look what they've done to you.'

'I'm okay.'

'Thank goodness,' she said.

'But I'm afraid this got damaged.' Jimmy opened his bag and took out *The Whistler*, handing it over to Miss Snow. 'I'm really sorry.'

'Don't you worry. It's not your fault. Anyway, it's only a little wet now,' she assured him. 'It'll be fine.'

'I'm really sorry,' Jimmy said again, thinking she'd never lend him any more of her plays ever again. 'I'll buy you another copy.'

'I've said it's fine. I wasn't going to read it again, anyway. It was for you.'

'For me?'

'I didn't expect you to give it back. It was a gift.'

'Oh,' Jimmy said. 'Thank you.'

'I'll put it here while it dries out,' she said, placing it on the arm of the chair nearest the fire. Even though it was late spring and quite mild, the fire was a comforting presence.

'I can't be long, I'm afraid,' Jimmy said, even though there was nothing he wanted to do more than stay in front of the fire, listening to it crackle, and slowly fall asleep. 'Mum will be worried if I'm out long.'

'What did you tell her?'

'That I was going to the bookshop.'

Miss Snow smiled. 'I guess I'll have to find another book for you, then, eh?'

'Oh, I didn't mean that,' Jimmy said, aghast that she might have thought he was after another freebie.

'Jimmy,' she said, 'I have nobody else I can share my books with.' She looked pensive for a moment. 'Well, except my granddaughter, but she only visits at weekends.' A pained looked crossed Miss Snow's face. 'I wish I saw more of her, but she's always so busy. She's at drama school.'

'An actress like you?'

Miss Snow nodded. 'Catherine – my daughter – wasn't too happy when she started to show signs of wanting to be an actress. Catherine's a very sensible lawyer, you see. But my granddaughter's been very successful. She's starred in all sorts of things.' Miss Snow shook her head. 'That's one of the awful things about the profession. Everybody adores you once you've made it – can't get enough of you then. But nobody supports you in the early days. It's always, *when are you going to get a proper job?*'

'My mum wants me to work in an office,' Jimmy

said.

Miss Snow looked at him. 'And what have you told her?'

'Nothing. I just keep the peace.'

She laughed. 'Very sensible of you, Jimmy.'

They were quiet for a few moments. Only the sound of the fire broke the silence and the comforting tick of a clock on the mantelpiece.

'Was it the same for you?' Jimmy asked at last.

'Wanting to become an actress?'

Jimmy nodded. 'Yes.'

'Worse – much worse. My father was terribly old-fashioned. He thought I should be nothing more than a wife and mother. The idea that I wanted a career – *any* career – was quite outrageous.'

'So, how did you become an actress?'

'Sheer determination,' Miss Snow laughed. 'I never gave up. It's the only way because there are a lot of knock-backs. And, of course, my father didn't speak to me for years. He was fine once my name was up in lights in the West End. Used to bring all his friends to see me. "That's my girl!" he'd shout when I'd come on stage. It was very embarrassing.'

Jimmy laughed.

'Talking of the West End,' Miss Snow continued, her eyes dancing with a merry light, 'I still keep in touch with some of my old theatre buddies in London.'

'Even though you're retired?'

'Oh, yes. Just because I'm hidden away here, it doesn't mean I don't know what's going on.' She paused. 'Have you heard of Ben Farley?'

'No,' Jimmy said.

'He's a director. Theatre mostly, with the

occasional independent film when he can get the money together.' Miss Snow paused again, as if to let Jimmy digest this information. 'I worked with him a few years ago – my last job, as a matter of fact – and I still keep in touch. He's a very sweet man. Talented to his fingertips, of course. Anyway,' she said. 'I heard from him last week. He's got a new show on in the West End: *Family Matters*. Have you heard of it?'

'Yes,' Jimmy said. 'I read it last year.'

'Then you'll know there's a part in it for a boy about your age.'

'Philip Tranter?'

'The very one.' Miss Snow's eyes sparkled with sudden mischief. 'Well?'

Jimmy looked at her. 'What?'

'Why don't you go up for it? Auditions are next Tuesday.'

Jimmy was dumbstruck. 'Me? Audition?'

'Why not?'

'I've never auditioned for anything real before – I mean, other than at school. I haven't got any experience.'

'And you never will have if you don't put yourself out there.'

Put yourself out there! He liked that phrase. He nodded, deep in thought. Jimmy Catesby as Philip Tranter. A West End debut. He might be discovered … he might become famous, he might – but he shouldn't get ahead of himself. He hadn't even auditioned yet.

'Would I have to prepare a scene from the play?'

'Of course,' Miss Snow said. 'I could find out which one, if you like?'

'Could you?' Jimmy asked.

Miss Snow nodded. 'I certainly could.'

Jimmy grinned, a great bubble of excitement growing in his stomach. But his smile suddenly faded.

'What is it?' Miss Snow asked.

'My mum. What will I tell my mum?'

Miss Snow nodded, looking anxious for a moment. 'Probably best not to tell her anything. Not just yet, anyway. It'll be our secret.'

Jimmy smiled again. Miss Snow was right. There was no point upsetting his mum when he might not even get the part.

'Is that settled, then?' Miss Snow asked.

Jimmy nodded. 'It'll be our secret,' he repeated.

5. THE AUDITION

Jimmy had never been into London on his own before. Miss Snow had given him some money for his ticket and for something to eat even though he'd said he had enough pocket money saved. She'd also given him a copy of the play and a map to The Countess Theatre near Piccadilly.

'It's the most beautiful theatre in London,' she'd told him, her eyes flooding with emotion. 'You probably won't see the actual stage, though. They normally hold auditions in some horrible draughty room at the back of the building.'

Jimmy didn't mind. This was the biggest adventure of his life. He could be auditioning in a broom cupboard for all he cared.

Pure excitement coursed through him as he caught the train that morning. He was meant to be in school, of course, and had left home as usual, saying bye to his mum and taking all his books with him. But there was something else in his rucksack that morning: a change of clothes. Miss Snow had it all planned out.

'You won't want to turn up in your school uniform, so come here instead of school and change clothes. You can leave your books with me and collect them later. You'll be back in plenty of time and your mum won't be any the wiser.'

Jimmy had changed into his favourite pair of jeans and a clean, sky blue shirt.

'Very smart,' Miss Snow told him.

She stood by the window and waved him off after telling him to, 'Break a leg!' Apparently, actors didn't wish each other good luck like other people.

Arriving at Piccadilly, Jimmy got his ticket ready for the barriers and tried to look as if he knew where he was going. There were so many exits. He stood still for a moment, looking around. Which one did he want? He looked at Miss Snow's map. *Look for Eros*, she'd written in spidery black writing. Jimmy glanced up and almost whooped for joy when he saw an exit marked, *Eros*. What Eros was, he had no idea but, climbing the steps up into the bustle of Piccadilly, he guessed it was the statue where all the tourists were having their picture taken.

He gave a low whistle as he looked around him. There were so many people and they all seemed to know exactly where they were going. He looked at the map. He needed to cross the road somewhere and then take a left. *It isn't far*, Miss Snow had assured him and, sure enough, after ten minutes of walking and getting lost, he was standing outside The Countess Theatre. Miss Snow was right – it was beautiful. Startlingly white, it had large columns and steps leading up to the entrance. There was also the biggest queue Jimmy had ever seen. It seemed to be snaking its way round the side of the building where it disappeared into a side door.

'Excuse me,' he said to a woman at the end of the queue. 'Is this the queue for the audition?'

'Yes,' she said and smiled. 'Are you here for one of the children's parts?'

Jimmy nodded as he took his place behind her.

'I'm here for the part of the mother.'

'Are you?'

She nodded. 'I'm Maggie.'

'Jimmy.'

'Pleased to meet you.'

She looked nice and Jimmy wondered if they were destined to become a theatrical family.

'I hope it doesn't rain,' she said, staring up at the sky which had darkened suddenly.

'How long do you think we'll have to wait?'

'I think they're going to let everyone in at once, but you never can tell how long they'll be.'

'I didn't realise there'd be so many people.'

'It's an open audition. It was advertised in the press so there's bound to be a lot of interest.'

Jimmy nodded and then peered down the long row of people in front of him. How many boys were there up for the part of Philip Tranter, he wondered? He looked along the queue, noting all the competition.

One was too old, Jimmy thought, looking at a boy standing a few feet away, so he must be up for the part of the older brother, Mark.

A second was too young-looking even for the part of Philip.

A third was rather tall, Jimmy thought. And a fourth was rather fat.

His eye caught somebody else near the front of the queue. He was about the same height and weight as Jimmy and the same age, he guessed. But, unlike Jimmy, he looked super-confident. Jimmy guessed that he must go to auditions all the time. He was probably a big star although Jimmy didn't recognise him.

He took a deep breath. What had he got himself into? This auditioning was a serious business. Maybe he should have stuck to drama classes at school. He felt safe there – he knew what he was doing and yet, at the same time, he knew he had to do this if he wanted to get anywhere. Directors didn't just drop by your school and ask if you wanted to be part of their play or film. In Miss Snow's words, you had to *put yourself out there.*

He wondered if his favourite actors had ever got nervous at auditions? Had James Stewart ever got the jitters and thought about legging it? Had Tom Hanks ever wondered what on earth he was doing? Somehow, Jimmy couldn't imagine it.

As if reading his mind, Maggie smiled. 'Nervous?'

Jimmy was so nervous that he could only nod in response.

'First time?'

He nodded again and watched as Maggie dug into her handbag and pulled out a chocolate-covered cereal bar. 'Here,' she said. 'It'll keep your strength up.'

'Oh, I couldn't,' Jimmy said.

'That's all right. I've got three more – look.' She showed Jimmy the contents of her handbag and he smiled.

'Thanks,' he said.

'You never know how long these days are going to be or how gruelling,' she said. 'Have you learnt your lines?'

'As best as I can,' Jimmy said.

'Want to read them through with me?'

'Would you mind?'

'Not at all. And you can help me with mine.'

Jimmy grinned and determined that he was going to enjoy this day as much as he could.

Another half hour passed before the side door was opened and the queue made a slow progress inside.

Jimmy and Maggie, who were now word perfect with their speeches, winked and grinned at each other.

'Well, here goes,' Maggie said, crossing her fingers.

They were ushered into the building, along a rather grim passageway and up some stairs into a large studio surrounded by mirrors. Now that everybody was inside, there didn't look like that many people really and Jimmy began to relax, watching as a tall man approached the group and held his hands up for silence. He was wearing blue jeans and a dark red shirt which was undone at the neck and his dark red wavy hair looked as if it hadn't been brushed for at least a month. Jimmy liked him instantly.

'Good morning everybody. Sorry for the delay. The room was in use and we couldn't get in, but we're ready to go now. My name's Ben Farley and I'll be the director of *Family Matters*. These are my assistants – Amy Havant and Diana Greig. If you have any questions during the day, feel free to approach us. Okay,' he said, clapping his hands together and bouncing up and down on his feet, 'this is the plan for today. The audition pieces we've asked you to prepare will be performed first. Once we've had a chance to hear those, the people we'd like to take forward will be put into family groups. As you know, we're looking for three sets of children and a lead mother and father plus understudies. It will be a pretty intensive day. There'll be an hour for lunch at twelve o'clock and we hope to finish by three.'

'Three?' Jimmy said in shock.

'That's pretty good,' Maggie told him.

'But I've got to be back by four.'

Maggie raised her eyebrows.

Jimmy shook his head. 'It's okay. I'll work

something out.'

'So,' Ben Farley ended, 'good luck everyone and enjoy yourselves.'

Everybody was ushered into an orderly queue outside the auditioning studio. There were a few seats, but not nearly enough. Jimmy was too excited to sit down. He couldn't even look at his script anymore. Maggie looked rather hyper too, he thought.

'This is the worst part,' she confided. 'You're nearly there, but not quite. It's a torturous limbo where you're not quite yourself, but not quite the character either.'

Jimmy nodded. She was succeeding in making him even more nervous than before. He watched as, one by one, the boys, girls, men and women were called into the studio, the door swinging shut behind them. It was impossible to hear anything that was said so Jimmy didn't bother trying. Instead, he tried to focus on his breathing as Miss Snow had told him to.

'An actor's voice is his ultimate tool and breath is its driving force. You must learn to breathe properly.'

Jimmy practised. Miss Snow and Miss Parnaby had taught him how and he did it whenever he could: walking to school, in between classes, first thing when he got out of bed and last thing at night.

'Wish me luck!' Maggie suddenly said.

Jimmy blinked. How had that happened so fast?

'Good lu- break a leg!' he remembered just in time.

Maggie beamed then disappeared through the door into the studio. Jimmy's heart was thumping wildly now. He was next and he didn't feel ready. A little voice inside him said he didn't have to do this. Why put yourself through this torture? Why not leave now? You could go round the shops. Hop on a bus and see some of London. Nobody would blame you.

I would!

Jimmy shook his head as if trying to dislodge such rebellious thoughts. He had to do this: not just for himself, but for Miss Snow too. She believed in him.

Before he could even contemplate running away again, Maggie came out of the studio. Her face was flushed red and she looked a little dazed.

'Are you okay?'

She nodded, but didn't say anything.

Jimmy watched as she walked away and, as much as he wanted to go and talk to her, he knew he had to walk through the door. It was his turn now and there was no going back.

'And you are?' Ben Farley asked, looking up from a table in the middle of the room where he sat with his two assistants. All of them had huge clipboards in front of them and copies of the play.

'Jimmy Catesby – James.'

Ben frowned for a moment. That surely wasn't a good sign, was it, Jimmy thought.

'You're Mary's friend, aren't you?'

Jimmy nodded. 'Yes.'

Ben grinned and Jimmy immediately relaxed. 'This young lad's a friend of Mary Snow's.'

His assistants looked impressed.

'So which scene are you going to read for us, Jimmy?' Amy Havant asked.

'The disagreement with Mark.'

'Good choice,' Ben said. 'I'll be Mark'

And they were off.

It was the strangest, most wonderful experience of Jimmy's life. He was, at once, nervous and exhilarated, petrified yet focused. The lines were a joy to read and he really felt the spirit of Philip Tranter entering him.

When he reached the end of the scene, he felt completely dazed by it all, almost as if coming round from a very deep sleep.

'Well,' Ben said, looking straight at Jimmy, 'that was quite a performance. Thank you for coming and we'll talk to you again later.'

Jimmy nodded. Was that it? Didn't they give you any more feedback than that? He'd just poured his very soul into a role and they were going to leave him dangling with a mere sentence-worth of response.

He walked out, still feeling stunned by the whole experience. What had happened to him in there? He'd never felt anything quite like it in his life. As soon as he'd started reading his lines, something had taken over him and Jimmy Catesby had ceased to be. It had been the strangest, most fantastic and completely addictive experience, and he knew he wanted more.

'Jimmy?'

He looked up and saw Maggie.

'How did it go?'

Jimmy shrugged. 'I'm not sure. Good, I think. How can you tell?'

'Your guts.'

'What do you mean?'

'How do you feel in your guts?'

Jimmy placed a hand on his belly. 'All churny and weird,' he said.

Maggie nodded. 'That's good.'

'Is it?'

'In my experience.'

'How did yours go?'

'Bad,' she said, 'very bad. I was terrible. I just didn't get into it, I'm afraid. And I *love* this role too. I can't understand what went wrong. But that's how it goes in this game.'

Jimmy's eyes widened. That sounded terrible. Maybe his audition hadn't gone as well as he'd thought. Maybe he was fooling himself – his mind was playing tricks on him as part of some kind of strange survival tactic.

'How long do you think we'll have to wait?' he asked.

Maggie shrugged. 'There's no telling, but they do seem to be moving everyone along at a fair pace. Fancy another cereal bar?'

Jimmy grinned and they both munched together in silence.

It was about forty minutes later when the door opened and Ben Farley ushered everybody into the studio. Jimmy and Maggie stood next to each other, glancing at one another nervously.

'Here goes,' she whispered.

'Firstly,' Ben said, clapping his hands together, 'I'd like to thank everybody for their patience today. I'd also like to thank you all for your performances. It's been a real pleasure meeting you all and I regret that we're only able to take a small percentage of you forward to this afternoon's auditions.'

At those words, Jimmy felt a surge of adrenalin. Was he amongst the small percentage or was he catching the next train home? He could barely breathe for nerves.

'I'm going to read some names out and I'd like those people to stand at this end of the studio,' Ben said, pointing to the far side.

'Gosh,' Maggie said, 'it's like that TV programme where they keep you in suspense for as long as possible.'

'Olivia Haynes, Lauren Lucas, Georgia Ware, Chris Newman …

The list went on. Jimmy's eyes were wide with fear.

'Matthew Stapleton, Maggie Owen.'

Maggie grabbed Jimmy's shoulder and gasped, leaving his side to join the others at the far side of the studio. Did that mean she'd made it through to the next round of auditions?

'James Catesby.'

Jimmy's heart flipped right over. He was going to join Maggie on the other side of the room. Was that good or bad?

Maggie grabbed his arm again as he joined her.

'And, finally, Joe Everard.'

The room had been divided although there seemed slightly fewer people on Jimmy's side of the studio.

'Thank you for your time, everyone. The people to my right will not be going forward to this afternoon's auditions.'

'Oh my goodness!' Maggie exclaimed.

'Which means you guys will be working hard again after lunch.'

'That's us. That's us! We've made it!' Maggie said.

Jimmy was dumbstruck. He couldn't believe it. He'd got through. Okay, so there were about thirty of them, but he was one of the chosen ones.

'I suggest,' Ben said, 'that you grab a bite to eat and be back here for one o'clock. That's when the really hard work will begin.'

Jimmy and Maggie left the studio with great fat

grins on their faces.

'I can't believe it,' Maggie said. 'I thought I'd done really badly.'

'You were wrong,' Jimmy said.

They left the theatre by the side door by which they'd entered. To Jimmy, it seemed an age since he'd been standing outside in the queue not knowing what to expect, and he felt like a different person.

'You okay?' Maggie asked. 'You're very quiet.'

'I don't think I really believe it yet.'

Maggie smiled at him. 'They're going to make us jump through hoops now.'

'What will we have to do?'

'I guess we'll have to read with some of the other actors. They'll be looking for people who look right for the roles at this stage.'

Jimmy panicked. He hadn't thought of that. Did he look like Philip Tranter? He hadn't noticed anything in the play about what Philip looked like. Dark hair or fair? Slim or fat? Were his eyes blue or brown?

'Don't worry,' Maggie told him. 'From my experience, they're usually more concerned about whether you have a feel for the character than what you look like.'

They walked down Shaftesbury Avenue, turning off into a small street.

'Come on,' Maggie said, 'I know just the place to get a spot of something to eat and it's good and cheap too.'

Jimmy breathed a sigh of relief. He'd already eaten the packed lunch his mum had made him for school and was ravenous now. He'd also heard what London prices could be like and had been worried that he wouldn't have enough for more than a can of cola.

Sure enough, Maggie's favoured café was cheap and cheerful and they bought a slice of pizza and a drink and sat at a table on the pavement, watching the world go by.

'I feel really naughty,' Jimmy confessed through a mouthful of pizza.

'You've got no worries – you'll burn the calories off in no time,' Maggie said.

'No – not the food – school.'

'What? You bunking off school, are you?'

'Of course.'

'Oh, I thought you'd be at one of those drama schools that lets you have time off for auditions.'

Jimmy's eyes narrowed. 'What?'

'Haven't you heard of drama schools?'

He shook his head. He'd heard Miss Snow mention that her granddaughter went to one, but he didn't know anything more than that.

'I went to one. They're pretty much like ordinary schools – you have to do all the boring subjects like English, maths and science and stuff, but they squeeze in loads of drama and dance and singing too. It's brilliant. They have their own agencies too and put their pupils up for auditions. Directors use them all the time and you have a real advantage if you go to them.'

Jimmy's mouth had dropped open in amazement. A drama school. It sounded fabulous.

'How do you get to be a pupil there?'

'Audition, of course, like anything else in this business.'

'Is it easy?'

Maggie laughed as she stirred some more sugar

into her coffee. 'Of course not. There aren't ever enough places for the people who want to get in and they come from all over the country.'

'But anyone can apply?'

Maggie nodded. 'They're horribly expensive, though. Thousands of pounds each year.'

Jimmy's heart sank. He'd thought it had sounded too good to be true. It wasn't enough to be talented and lucky, you also had to be very, very rich.

'There are scholarships, though,' Maggie added.

'What are they?'

'They're for promising pupils who can't afford the fees. There aren't many scholarships, though, and the competition is fierce.'

But they existed, Jimmy thought. They existed and he wanted one.

6. ROUND TWO

It's morning in the Tranter household and Mark and Philip are at the breakfast table.
Mark: (whispering) I think they're going to get a divorce.
Philip: What?
Mark: Shush!
Philip: (whispering) What makes you say that?
Mark: Dad was on the phone again to that Marianne woman from work.
Philip: That doesn't mean anything. He talks to lots of women at work.
Mark: Yeah. Makes you wonder.
Philip: You don't know what you're talking about.
Mark: I know a good deal more than you.
Philip: Just because you're older, doesn't mean you're smarter.
Mark: I could knock your brains out, little bro, so you'd better not speak to me like that again.
Philip: (frowning, as if he's about to thump Mark) God, you're so basic.
Mark: What do you mean?
Philip: You're like an animal that's-

'Okay,' Ben interrupted.

Jimmy blinked as he stopped in mid-sentence. Had they done it all wrong? He'd thought he'd performed okay.

'I'd like to try Philip – er – Jimmy?'

Jimmy nodded.

'I'd like you to read with Chris as Mark.' Ben beckoned to a boy at the other end of the studio. It was ten past two and, since lunch, they'd been reading in pairs. Jimmy had read with three other boys now and he could do the script without looking.

'Hi,' a voice said. 'I'm Chris.'

'I'm Jimmy,' he said, looking up into a face about two feet above his. This boy was huge!

'Hey! That's incredible,' Ben said. 'Amy, Diana – look at this.'

The ladies broke off from their groups at opposite ends of the studio and came over.

'Are you two brothers for real?' Diana asked.

Jimmy grinned, taking in the startling similarity between him and Chris for the first time. Other than Chris's tremendous size, he had the same dark, tousled hair and bright blue eyes. He even had a smattering of freckles over his nose.

'Okay, well you both look like brothers – let's see what you can do,' Ben said, and they read the scene together. This time, there was no interruption and they read to the end of the scene which was a great relief to Jimmy because he liked to finish things properly. It didn't seem right to leave a scene hanging unfinished.

They were then asked to sit on a bench at the far side of the room.

'You do this sort of thing often?' Chris asked Jimmy.

'No,' he said. 'First time.'

'Blimey.'

'What?' Jimmy asked.

'You're good.'

'You think so?'

Chris nodded. 'Yeah.'

'I thought you were good too,' Jimmy said.

'You did?'

'Yes. Do you go to drama school?'

'No way. I saw this advertised in the paper and

thought it would be a laugh.'

Jimmy smiled. To him, this audition represented his life's dreams yet to Chris it was just a laugh.

'Still want to get through, though,' Chris said. 'I left school last year and haven't found a decent job. You know – something I really want to do. I've been working in this fast food place down the road from me. It really sucks. I don't want to be stuck there for the rest of my life. You go to drama school, then?' Chris asked.

'I'd like to,' Jimmy said, 'I go to Penham High.'

Chris's eyebrows rose. 'Really? My-'

'Okay!' Ben interrupted again. It seemed to be his favourite occupation. 'Can we have all the fathers and mothers over with Amy, all the Kates with Diana over there, and all the Marks and Philips here with me. If you'll bear with us, we'll try not to take too long.'

Once they were in their groups, they were paired up again. Jimmy and Chris were still a pair which pleased Jimmy as he felt an automatic bond with Chris – very much as he had done with Miss Snow.

Then chaos reigned as everybody was asked to read at once. The whole room was filled with voices as each pair read through their scene. Jimmy's ears rang with words, but he did his best to shut them out and concentrate on his part. Chris was well into his. He was so convincing in his role as big brother Mark that Jimmy felt goosebumps down his back.

'Blimey,' Jimmy said once they'd finished the scene.

'What?' Chris asked.

'That was good, wasn't it?'

'I think so.'

They grinned at each other and Jimmy felt as if he'd known Chris all his life.

'Shall we go again?' Chris asked.

'You bet.'

And off they went.

'All RIGHT!' Ben Farley shouted above the noise when Jimmy and Chris were half-way through their scene for the third time. Everyone was silent again apart from a few nervous titters around the room. 'That was really crazy. Well done, everyone. We're just about there. Er – Amy?'

Ben's assistant, Amy Havant, stepped forward. She had curly blonde hair and a bright face that seemed to smile at everyone all at once. Ben and Diana passed over a sheet of paper each.

'This is the moment of truth,' Chris whispered to Jimmy and he gulped.

Amy began. 'I'm going to read some names out now so please listen carefully for yours.'

It was a wonder that Jimmy could hear anything because his heart was thump-thumping in his ears. He strained to listen as she read from a list in her hand. He thought he heard his name a couple of times:

'Jim Harrington.'

'James Cleaver.'

His name wasn't there. And neither was Chris's.

'Okay,' Amy said at last. 'I'm afraid those people haven't got through on this occasion and will be leaving us now. But well done for getting so far and many thanks for your time today. And, of course, that means that the rest of you will be cast in the show.'

Jimmy's mouth gaped open in a big black hole and, before he knew what was happening, he was being swung around by a crazy Chris who was whooping and wailing in delight.

'I don't believe it,' Chris shouted. 'It must be a joke.'

Jimmy laughed. He couldn't believe it either. He'd made it. He'd got his first big break. He was going to be an actor in a West End play. Nothing like this had ever happened to him before and he was so excited by it all.

'If you're going to dream, dream big!' Miss Snow had told him. Well, he felt as if he was dreaming big now. As long as he didn't ever have to wake up.

Jimmy looked around the room. Everybody was wearing ecstatic grins as if they'd got all their birthdays and Christmases at once.

Chris was digging round in his pocket and brought out a mobile phone. Jimmy didn't like to earwag, but couldn't help watching Chris's face as he passed on his good news to somebody.

'Okay!' A voice suddenly cut through the excitement. 'We've got a lot of boring administrative stuff to get through now,' Diana Greig said.

Forms and pens were handed out along with copies of the script. Ben, Amy and Diana went around and talked to everyone about the demands of rehearsals which were starting the very next week. Ben was the one who spoke to Jimmy.

'Well done,' he said, shaking his hand. 'Mary Snow's judgement never fails. She'll be proud of you, I'm sure.'

'Thank you, Mr Farley,' Jimmy said politely.

'I think you can call me Ben now,' he said smiling. 'As you know, we've hired understudies today, but I particularly wanted you and Chris as the brothers. I know you'll do a great job. It'll be a lot of hard work and you'll have to make sure you don't miss rehearsals.'

Jimmy nodded, knowing full well that the Easter holidays started next week which meant three weeks off school. If rehearsals went on any longer, he'd have to find some way of attending, even if it meant skipping school and getting into trouble with everyone.

'We're still deciding on which actors to form family groups, but it's pretty certain you and Chris will be together.'

And then it was all over. Chris and Jimmy swapped phone numbers before they left.

'Where do you live?' Jimmy asked him, curious to find out more about the chap who was going to play his big brother.

'Camden,' Chris said. 'Got a room with my brother and his mates. Five of us in a two-bedroomed flat.' He laughed and Jimmy laughed too even though it sounded rather grim to him. Still, it must be fun living without a mum to fuss around you all the time, he thought. Jimmy watched Chris sauntering out of the studio. He made everything look so casual as if nothing ever fazed him. Then, looking at his watch, Jimmy almost had a heart attack. He had to get home. He was just opening the studio door when he almost crashed into a young girl.

'Sorry!' he blurted.

The girl stared at him as though she was about to say something like, *Idiot*, to him. Still, he couldn't help noticing how pretty she was. She had the longest hair he had ever seen and it was the colour of vanilla ice-cream. He wracked his brains for something intelligent to say, but his mind was a perfect – or *im*perfect – blank and, before he had the chance to marshal some sensible words into his mouth, she'd gone.

As he left the theatre, he wondered who the girl with vanilla hair was. He hadn't noticed her during the auditions. Still, that wasn't surprising as there'd been so much to take in. It had been the most bizarre day of his life and he still felt completely bowled over by it. As he walked along the street, he didn't hear the roar of the traffic. He didn't hear the honking horns or the sirens of a police car as it sped by. He didn't notice the delicious smell of pizza and hamburgers wafting towards him from a nearby restaurant, and he almost didn't hear Maggie.

'JIMMY!' she shouted again.

He turned around. 'Maggie! I thought you'd gone.'

'Couldn't go without congratulating you. You've done brilliantly.'

Jimmy blushed. 'Thanks.

'How does it feel?' she asked.

'I'm not sure,' he said. 'It feels weird. Like I'm floating or something.'

Maggie laughed. 'Don't forget it. It's a once in a lifetime experience and you deserve it.'

He smiled. He did feel great. He felt as if the whole world was on his side – rooting for him and slapping him on the back.

'How about you?' Jimmy suddenly asked, almost forgetting his manners. When Amy Havant had been reading the names out, he'd been so wrapped up in his own world that he hadn't noticed when Maggie's name had been called out and hadn't remembered seeing her much after lunch.

She shook her head.

'What?' Jimmy asked.

'Not this time, darling,' she said.

'You didn't make it?'

She shook her head and then leant forward and kissed him on the cheek before turning and disappearing into the crowd. Jimmy stood staring after her. It was the second time that day that he hadn't known what to say.

7. KEEPING MUM

'Jimmy Catesby!' Miss Snow chastised him as he entered the hallway of Penham Manor. 'You were meant to ring me!'

'I know,' Jimmy said. 'I'm sorry. I don't know what happened. I kinda lost track of time.'

'Well, *I* know what happened,' Miss Snow said. 'You got the part and went into what I refer to as *stage stupor.*'

'How did you know?'

She smiled. 'Because you've got that look about you. You *did* get the part, didn't you?'

Jimmy nodded and Miss Snow gave a whoop of joy which seemed very unfeminine and made him laugh.

'I KNEW you would!' she said in delight. 'And Ben. What did you make of Ben?'

'He's great.'

'Isn't he?'

'He knew who I was.'

'Of course.'

'You rang him, didn't you?'

'I did.'

'Is that why I got the part?'

She frowned. 'Jimmy! Of *course* not. I only put in a good word for you. In this game, you need all the help you can get, but you have to survive on your own. I can't audition for you so you must have done perfectly well on your own.'

Jimmy flushed with pride at her words.

They walked through to the living room where Jimmy's school books and uniform were.

'I'd better get changed.'

'I'll get you a drink and something to eat,' Miss Snow said, letting him dress in private.

'What play were you in with Ben?' Jimmy called through to the kitchen as he took off his best clothes and put his school uniform back on again.

'The last play was called *Summer*,' Miss Snow replied as she clanked about with the teapot and a biscuit tin. 'It was a romantic comedy. It was quite successful. Ben wanted to turn it into a film, but it all fell through. I think it would make a lovely film.'

'And you worked with him on films too?'

'Yes,' Miss Snow said, appearing at the door. '*Lying to Michael*, and *Winter Fortune*.'

'Oh,' Jimmy said disappointedly. 'I haven't seen those.'

'Not surprising. They were tiny films and only shown in a few cinemas, but Ben's a real talent. His time will come.'

Jimmy smiled. He could feel a deep stirring which told him that he wanted to be around when that happened.

'When do you start rehearsals?' Miss Snow asked, bringing the tea things into the living room.

'Next week.'

'So you'll be on holiday, won't you?'

Jimmy nodded.

'What do you think your mother will say?'

Jimmy sighed. 'I don't think I should tell her.'

'Is that wise? She's going to find out. How on earth can you keep it a secret?'

'I'll say I'm round a friend's.'

'Every day for all those weeks?'

Jimmy shrugged. 'She'll be working most of the

time anyway. She'll think I'm at home.'

Miss Snow frowned. 'I can't say I feel happy about that.'

For a moment, Jimmy wanted to cross the room and hug her. She was so sweet and she seemed to have cast herself in the role of Jimmy's surrogate grandmother.

'Don't worry,' he said, 'if she gets suspicious, I'm a pretty good actor and she usually believes me.'

Miss Snow chuckled. 'I don't doubt that for a moment.'

Jimmy left Penham Manor and ran down Main Street, through the village and on towards home as fast as his feet would carry him. As he entered his road, he saw that his mum's car was in the driveway – the old Volkswagen Polo that had seen better days ten years ago. Immediately he felt his nerves get the better of him. He'd been performing well all day in his auditions, but could he pull the wool over his mum's eyes?

As soon as he was through the front door, she fell upon him like a vulture.

'JAMES CATESBY!' she yelled. 'I've been worried sick. Where have you been all this time? And don't you dare tell me the bookshop because I went there on my way home.'

'I was at a friend's,' he said in a very small voice.

'What friend?'

'Chris?'

'Never heard of him.'

'He's a new friend, Mum.'

'Well, where does this Chris live?'

Jimmy's thoughts stumbled for a moment. He

couldn't very well say Camden, could he?

'He lives the other side of the village,' he said. Well, that was kind of true, wasn't it?

'You've got a phone, Jimmy. You should've called me. What did I get you a phone for if you never have it on or check it for messages?'

'Sorry, Mum. The time just flew by.'

'Not for me it didn't. I was about to call the police. I nearly rang the school.'

Jimmy's heart skipped a beat. Thank goodness she hadn't.

'I promise I'll ring in the future.'

'*If* I let you out of my sight in the future,' his mum chastised.

Jimmy went up to his room in disgrace, wondering if he could possibly move in with Chris, his brother and the rest of the gang in Camden. Surely it had to be better than living with his mother.

He was forgiven by teatime when his mum served him a plate full of buttery scrambled eggs, beans on toast, bacon and a mug of hot chocolate – all of which he wolfed down in record time. Other than a ginger biscuit at Miss Snow's, he hadn't had anything since the slice of pizza at lunch time in London and that seemed an age ago.

'How was school?' his mum asked. Why did parents always ask kids that, Jimmy wondered? Was it because they missed it so much themselves or because they couldn't think of anything else to say?

'Fine,' Jimmy said between mouthfuls of bacon and beans. 'How was work?' It was Jimmy's way of deflecting attention away from himself. He was far happier as a listener than as a talker and his mum could talk for England. Sure enough, she launched into the latest saga of office life which involved a work colleague called Tracey and a stationery supplier called Bob.

Jimmy managed to zone out as his mother talked, nodding occasionally in what he hoped were the right places, but his mind was back in the studio where the auditions had been held. He thought of Maggie and how kind she'd been and wondered what she'd do now. He thought of Ben and his messy hair and great enthusiasm. He thought of Chris and how talented he was. And he thought of the girl with the vanilla hair.

'He's married, you know,' his mum was saying. 'Not that Tracey has any scruples about that. *All's fair in love and stationery*, she says. Isn't that an attitude?'

Jimmy nodded.

'Are you listening to me? Jimmy?'

Jimmy suddenly realised that his mum was speaking to him. 'What?'

'You haven't heard a single word I've said.'

'Yes I have,' Jimmy protested.

'What have I been talking about, then?'

Jimmy frowned. Think. Rewind. 'Tracey,' he said triumphantly.

'What about her?'

Goodness. His mum wasn't usually really bothered if he listened or not. What had got into her tonight? 'Tracey?'

'Yes!'

'She's – er – in trouble again.' It was a safe bet. Since his mum had started working at that office, he'd heard nothing, but Tracey this and Tracey that. She'd crashed cars, lost handbags, got drunk and fallen down an escalator – you name it and Tracey had done it. 'Yes – in trouble,' Jimmy finished lamely.

'Oh, you are funny,' she laughed, ruffling his hair as if he was four years old. 'Go and get your homework done,' she said and, rather relieved that he'd been let off the hook, Jimmy left the table.

Once upstairs, he unpacked his audition clothes and put them in his wardrobe. He'd sneak them into the wash after the weekend when his mum wouldn't remember what he'd worn. Then he took out his copy of the script.

'Highlight your own parts if you like,' Ben had told them, 'and feel free to make any notes you want on the pages. These scripts are yours.'

Wow, Jimmy thought. His first professional script. He wanted to sleep with it under his pillow, it was so precious. Perhaps that wasn't such a bad idea. At least it would be hidden from his mum when she came in to say goodnight later on.

He flipped through the pages, excited by the number of lines he'd have to learn. Some people might be daunted by them all but, to Jimmy, they were simply delicious: a wonderful feast to wrap his tongue around and he couldn't wait to step on stage and act them out.

Placing the script under his pillow, Jimmy settled down, but not to do his homework because he hadn't been in school that day. Instead, he got a piece of notepaper and wrote – in his very best handwriting:

Jimmy was absent from school today owing to an emergency trip to the dentist after a night of roaring toothache.

Yours sincerely

Fiona Catesby

He read it back to himself. It wasn't too over the top, was it? No. Old Mrs Huddlestone, his form tutor, never paid them much attention anyway. They were just stuck into the register.

'You in bed, Jimmy?' his mum said, knocking on his door some time later. 'You washed and brushed already?

'Yes, Mum.'

She popped her head round the door.

'Homework done?'

'Yes.'

'Need me to check anything?'

'Er – no, thank you.'

'What did you have to do?'

'Write a story,' Jimmy said.

'You're good at telling stories, aren't you?' his mum said.

'I hope so,' Jimmy said with a little smile.

There weren't many school days that Jimmy looked forward to, but Friday was one of them because it meant drama club at lunchtime. After a horrendously long lesson of double maths in which Jimmy managed to get every single decimal point in the wrong place, drama was complete bliss.

As usual, only the eight regulars turned up in the drama studio. Miss Parnaby was there, sitting in the middle of the floor with her long legs crossed like a Buddha. You wouldn't find the biology teacher sitting like that in the middle of the lab, nor the English teacher in her oh-so-prim tweed skirts, Jimmy thought. It was one of the things he loved about drama – it was all so relaxed. You could be yourself. You didn't have to worry about being correct all the time.

Another thing he liked about Miss Parnaby was that she didn't make them do anything silly. The drama teacher before Miss Parnaby had been very strange. She'd made them pretend to be trees and fish and stuff like that which Jimmy thought was a complete waste of time, and she never seemed to listen to suggestions which, Jimmy believed, was a big part of drama. No, Mrs Feasy hadn't been popular and, when she'd announced she was leaving, the whole class had cheered which had meant a break time detention when they'd had to pretend to be fish again. Miss Parnaby never pulled any stunts like that.

'Okay, everyone. Sit down and just close your eyes for a moment. We're going to focus on your breathing – slow, deep breaths – in from the nose and out through the mouth.'

Jimmy followed her lead and felt his body and mind begin to relax.

'Empty your minds. There is nothing to think about except you and your breathing. Now, when you're ready, I want you to stand up slowly, still with your eyes closed. Slowly and carefully.'

Jimmy positioned his feet and legs and, using his arms for balance, got up slowly.

'Now, still taking deep breaths, slowly open your eyes.'

Jimmy and the rest of the class did so, some exchanging smiles across the circle they'd made.

'Okay,' Miss Parnaby said at last. 'We're ready to start.'

Jimmy smiled. He felt relaxed and focussed and ready for anything. Miss Parnaby's exercises were great and there was nothing remotely fishy about them.

After a session of improvisation work on the theme of family conflict which Jimmy found particularly useful in preparation for his role in *Family Matters*, he decided to tell Miss Parnaby about his adventures in the West End.

'Jimmy – that's great news!' she said. 'I didn't know you were auditioning for plays.'

'Neither did I,' Jimmy said. 'It was kind of sudden.'

'But how are you going to attend rehearsals? Don't you need some sort of release form from school?'

'I don't know,' Jimmy said. Maybe that had been mentioned to him at the auditions. He'd been so hyper that he really couldn't remember.

'You'll need permission from the school, I think. Someone will have to sign it for you, I believe.'

'Will you do that for me, Miss?' Jimmy blurted.

Miss Parnaby frowned. 'I don't think I can, Jimmy, as much as I'd like to. It's probably for the headmaster or your form tutor. And won't your mum have to know? How does she feel about it?'

Jimmy lowered his eyes.

'She does know, doesn't she?' Miss Parnaby asked. 'Jimmy?'

He looked up. He couldn't lie to her even if he made believe that he was 'acting'. Miss Parnaby was his drama teacher and she'd be able to see right through him.

'I haven't told her yet.'

'But you'll have to – and sooner rather than later.'

'I will,' Jimmy said, thinking he'd delay it for as long as possible.

'But that's really brilliant. I'm so proud of you. And perhaps we could read through some of your scenes in drama club.'

Jimmy grinned. 'That would be great.'

There was a sudden loud knocking on the drama

studio door which led out into the playground. Jimmy turned around and saw Stoner and Wicks.

Miss Parnaby strutted over and opened the door. 'There are students working in here and, if you don't want to join in yourselves, I suggest you leave now.'

'Join in?' Stoner said with a nasty laugh. 'Not likely! Won't catch me in poncy tights.'

Wicks laughed, showing a snarl of ugly teeth, before spitting on the path.

Miss Parnaby slammed the door. Her face was flushed and she looked deeply annoyed.

'You all right, Miss?'

She nodded. 'What is wrong with those two?'

Jimmy rolled his eyes. 'Everything,' he said.

8. BIG BROTHER

Mr Crombie, the geography teacher, had a nasty habit of walking up and down the classroom and stopping to peer over your shoulders as you worked. Jimmy found it most unnerving particularly as he usually managed to get into an awful muddle with geography. He just couldn't get interested in crop rotation in the eighteenth century, or rain forest canopies or igneous rocks. So he doodled in the back of his book. It wasn't anything particularly artistic – just a collection of spirals and stars and-

'What are you doing, boy?' Mr Crombie suddenly bellowed in his unnaturally deep voice which made him sound just like one of rocks that he was always barking on about.

'Nothing, Sir,' Jimmy said, but it was too late – Crombie had hold of his exercise book and was examining the back page.

'Who is Philip Tranter?' Crombie barked.

Every pair of eyes in 7B was on Jimmy.

'Jimmy's boyfriend, Sir,' some smart alec at the front of the class shouted out.

'Quiet! I didn't ask for your opinion, did I?' Crombie said, glaring at the boy. 'Well?'

'Nobody, Sir.'

'What do you mean, nobody?'

'It's just a name, Sir.'

'It's a name you'll be writing out a hundred times after school tonight,' Crombie barked.

So Jimmy was late leaving school on Friday and didn't get a head start on Stoner and Wicks who were waiting for him by the village green.

'Well, well,' Stoner said, 'look who it is.'

'It's Tights Boy,' Wicks said.

'And he's been keeping us waitin', hasn't he? There's a price to pay for keeping us waitin', ain't there?'

Before he could react, they'd dragged him up an alley at the side of one of the cottages, ripped his rucksack off his back and had thrown him to the ground.

Jimmy felt a rage burning through him and he scrambled up to face Stoner but, although his anger gave him strength, he still wasn't strong enough to beat Stoner and he was back on the ground before he knew it with Stoner's huge foot in the middle of his back.

'So, what do we do with him now?' Stoner asked and Jimmy could imagine his ugly eyes narrowed and his thick lips snarling.

'We could see if he's got tights on again,' Wicks suggested.

'Nah. We did that last time. Want to make it more interestin' for him, don't we?' Stoner said, pushing his great foot into Jimmy's back. 'What's it like bein' teacher's pet, eh? We saw you all nice an' cosy with that stuck up drama teacher. We don't like her, do we?'

'Nah,' Wicks said.

'Shall I tell you what we did?'

Wicks gave a laugh which sounded like a blocked drain clearing. 'We broke her windscreen wipers on that stupid car of hers.'

'Slashed her tyres too. That'll teach her for being so stuck up.' Stoner gave Jimmy a kick in his lower back and, for one awful moment, Jimmy thought he was going to faint, but his anger was keeping him conscious and he wished, with all his heart, that he could get up and thump the living daylights out of both of them.

'Why don't we drop him into the river?' Wicks suddenly said. 'See if he can swim.'

Stoner gave an evil laugh.

Jimmy could feel his heart beat accelerate. He could swim but, if he knew Stoner and Wicks, they wouldn't just chuck him into the shallow part of the river, and Jimmy knew that you could drown a giraffe in the deep part.

'Get up, Tights Boy,' Stoner said, grabbing Jimmy's arm and yanking him up off the ground. 'We're goin' swimmin'.'

'HEY! Let him go!' a voice suddenly yelled.

Jimmy tried to look around, but couldn't and the next thing he knew Stoner was being ripped away from him. He heard Stoner's body being slammed up against the wall of the nearby cottage.

'What DO you think you're doing?' the stranger's voice shouted.

Jimmy, catching his breath, turned. It wasn't a stranger; it was Chris. What on earth was Chris doing there? But he didn't have time to ask.

'CHRIS!' Jimmy shouted as Wicks approached him from behind. Chris turned and sent Wicks flying with the merest tap of his foot against Wicks' leg. How on earth had he done that, Jimmy wondered, watching in awe as Wicks struggled for breath as he landed flat on the ground, crushing his nose under the weight of his own body.

'I was talking to you,' Chris said calmly, turning his attention back to Stoner whose neck he gripped in a vice-like fist. 'Eh? Are you deaf as well as stupid?'

'I wasn't doin' nuffin.'

'What?'

'I said I wasn't-'

'I *heard* what you said. It was your appalling English I couldn't understand.'

Chris turned to Jimmy. 'They can't even speak proper English.' Chris laughed, but then he turned serious. 'If I EVER hear that either of you have been picking on Jimmy – or anybody else – you'll be very sorry indeed. Do you understand me?'

There was silence for a moment as Stoner narrowed his mean eyes at Chris.

'I SAID, *do you understand?*'

Stoner nodded in defeat.

'You didn't know he had a big brother, did you?' Chris said.

Jimmy blinked. Boy, how he wished Chris really was his big brother. He sometimes thought his mum was incredibly selfish in making him an only child but, then again, since his father had left them when he was just three years old, there was only his mum to look after him and he knew he could be more than a handful at times.

Chris didn't let Stoner go immediately, but he couldn't keep him there forever and finally let go, watching in disgust as Stoner and Wicks walked away.

'Blimey!' Jimmy whistled. 'That was amazing.'

Chris smiled. 'All part of the service, little bro. Are you all right?'

Jimmy nodded. His back and right shoulder were a bit sore and his trouser knees were scuffed, but he was okay.

'Does that happen a lot?'

Jimmy didn't know what to say. He didn't want to come across as a wimp. 'Now and again,' he said, and then grinned. 'I didn't recognise you. It was like a superhero had taken possession of your body.'

'I'm not just a great actor, you know. I do have hidden talents,' Chris said.

Jimmy shook his head in astonishment. 'I wish you were around all the time.'

'I'm hoping I won't need to be after that. But, if you have any more trouble from them, let me know. I'm only a train ride away.'

'What are you doing here?'

'My cousin lives here,' Chris said.

'In Penham?'

'Yeah. I was trying to tell you at the audition, but we got interrupted. She goes to your school. Sarah Taylor.'

'Really?'

Chris nodded. 'You know her?'

'I've seen her,' Jimmy said, thinking of the blonde bombshell in year ten who'd never notice a lowly year seven pupil like him.

Suddenly, Jimmy had a brilliant idea. 'Hey! Have you ever heard of Mary Snow?'

'The actress?'

'Yes.'

'Sure. She was quite a babe in her time.'

Jimmy blushed. It was strange to hear her described like that. 'Well, you can meet her if you like.'

Chris's eyebrows rose. 'What do you mean – I thought she was dead.'

'No,' Jimmy said aghast. 'She lives here.'

'What, in Penham?'

Jimmy nodded excitedly. 'She's a friend and I can go over any time I like. Come on.'

After a quick phone call to his mum to assure her he'd be home for tea, Jimmy led Chris to Penham Manor. He felt strangely proud walking down the road with Chris and couldn't wait to introduce him and Miss Snow. He had the feeling that they'd like each other enormously.

A few minutes later, they were standing outside Miss Snow's. Jimmy peered in through the window. It looked unusually dark which was strange because Miss Snow normally kept at least one lamp on whatever the time of day. He knocked on the door and they waited. And waited.

'Maybe she's out,' Chris said.

'No, she never goes out.'

'How does she do her shopping?'

'She has a lady visit twice a week to make sure everything's okay.'

Jimmy knocked again. He was getting worried now. She was quite old, wasn't she? Certainly, she was the oldest person he'd ever known, and old people could fall over, couldn't they? She might have tumbled down the stairs or fallen over somewhere. She might, at this very moment, be lying with a broken hip, or arm or leg.

Jimmy knocked again. And then, as if in answer to a silent prayer, the door was opened and the pale white face of Miss Snow appeared.

'Jimmy!' she said in astonishment, as if he was the last person she'd expected to see.

'Miss Snow. I was worried – you didn't answer-'

'I was asleep,' she said, giving a little yawn. 'I fell asleep after lunch and seem to have forgotten to wake up. Very unlike me to sleep for longer than half an hour or so.'

'Are you all right?' Jimmy asked.

'Of course I'm all right apart from forgetting my manners – come in. Come in.'

'I've brought a friend, Miss Snow – this is Chris Newman. He's in the play.'

'Your older brother?'

'Yes. How did you guess?'

'He looks just like you,' Miss Snow said. 'Well, a little bigger.'

'Pleased to meet you, Miss Snow,' Chris said, shaking her frail hand in his strong one. He was about twice the height of her and twice as wide too. They looked like a giant and a doll and Chris had to duck to avoid the old beams which ran across the ceiling as he followed her inside.

Once seated with mugs of hot chocolate and a plate of sugary biscuits, they talked and talked.

They talked about food.

'I can eat a whole packet of biscuits in a sitting,' Chris said.

'I can believe that,' Miss Snow said.

They talked about Ben Farley.

'He once dressed up as Marilyn Monroe to sing "Happy Birthday" to me.' Miss Snow laughed. 'But don't tell him I told you.'

They talked about films.

'I like thrillers,' Chris said.

'I like romantic comedies,' Miss Snow said.

'I like anything,' Jimmy said.

And they talked about the theatre.

'It's the strangest profession in the world,' Miss Snow said. 'Pretending to be somebody else that is.

It's quite nutty when you think about it.'

Jimmy and Chris laughed.

'You forget yourself when you act,' Chris said. 'I like that. You become another person and you forget about yourself.'

Jimmy nodded. That was the part he liked best. He could forget about school and Stoner and Wicks as he took on a different life.

'But it's important for you boys to remember to constantly challenge yourselves. You mustn't become typecast. Do comedies as well as tragedies, musicals as well as drama, sitcoms and films. Change is the lifeblood of an actor.'

'I'd love to be in a film,' Jimmy said.

'Me too. Action hero,' Chris said.

'And after what you did to Stoner and Wicks, I know you'd be brilliant,' Jimmy said and then bit his lip.

'Who are Stoner and Wicks?' Miss Snow asked.

Jimmy glanced at Chris who cleared his throat. 'Oh, just a story I was telling Jimmy.'

Miss Snow nodded. Tactfully, she moved the conversation on. 'You know, you sometimes feel that the great writers have written parts just for you. Shakespeare, Chekhov, Shaw, Wilde. And you make them yours – you own the parts and it becomes very tough to pass them on and allow another actor to claim them as theirs.'

'What are your favourite parts?' Jimmy asked.

'Don't you mean, what *were* my favourite parts?' Miss Snow said with a smile. 'Oh, all the classics: Lady Macbeth, Juliet, Viola, Lady Bracknell. But I won't be playing them again.' She laughed. 'Aging is particularly difficult for actresses. To have played

Ophelia in *Hamlet* in one's youth and then to be asked to play Hamlet's mother, Gertrude, well, it's the harshest way of acknowledging the passage of time.'

'What was your worst experience on stage?' Chris asked.

Miss Snow's pale grey eyes glinted with mischief. 'I think it was the time I played a character called Melody in a truly terrible play called *Melody Sings*. I had to wear this appalling blonde wig which made me look like Barbie. It was so hot and scratchy. Most unpleasant. Well, one night, I was in the middle of this scene when I suddenly felt wonderfully cool and I couldn't work out why until the audience started laughing and I realised my wig had got caught on something and had come right off.'

'What happened?' Jimmy asked.

'They dropped the curtain, but I refused to have the wig put back on and so they had to brush my own hair into place and, when I went back on, I got a huge round of applause.'

'Did you ever get any bad reviews?' Chris asked.

'Chris!' Jimmy said, feeling very protective of Miss Snow.

'It's all right. I don't mind talking about that. I think actors should own the criticism as well as the praise – if it's deserved, that is. And, yes, I did get some terrible reviews. One of my first performances – as Titania in *A Midsummer Night's Dream* – was truly horrendous. Opening nights are an experience I shall never forget. The fear that runs through you is like nothing you'll experience anywhere else. It can drive a performance, of course, or it can ruin one. Unfortunately, it ruined mine and I was described as being "A youth with neither talent nor beauty to commend her".'

'But that's not true,' Jimmy shouted in outrage. 'You were beautiful as Ophelia.'

Miss Snow laughed. 'But not talented?'

'I didn't mean-'

'I'm just teasing. Thank you for your vote of confidence, Jimmy. Anyway, you'll be pleased to hear that I made that critic eat his words when he saw my Joan of Arc. He said I was "the most gifted young lady in theatre-land". I think he must have forgotten about my earlier performance. But that's the way of the theatre. You must take the highs with the lows.'

'So how come you're retired?' Chris asked.

'Old age, my dear boy. I'm afraid I get so tired these days although a lot of my contemporaries are still making films. It's not for me, though. I think you have to be young to fully enjoy it.'

'Who did you star with?' Chris said. He was beginning to sound like a chat show host with a list of questions to get through.

Miss Snow looked thoughtful for a moment. 'Let me see,' she began. 'I was lucky enough to be in Hollywood during the forties and fifties. Some say that was the golden age. I was with MGM for a while, but only ever had small walk-on parts although I was in *Cover Girl* with Gene Kelly and Rita Hayworth-'

'Did you get to dance with Gene Kelly?' Jimmy interrupted.

'Not on film, I'm afraid. But I did at a party once.' Her eyes glazed over for a moment. 'Ah, yes,' she said enigmatically. 'Quite a man. And I was one of the many actresses who tested for the role of Scarlet O'Hara in *Gone With the Wind.* I would've been completely wrong, though. Sometimes, you have to realise that you're just not cut out for every role. But I did quite well out of Hollywood. I was an extra in many other films too – with Elizabeth Taylor, Cary Grant-

Jimmy almost choked on his biscuit. Cary Grant was one of his heroes.

'- Doris Day. But I never quite made it as a lead. I don't regret a moment, though. I think I was far more suited to small British films and, as soon as I got my first lead back here, I was promptly nominated for an Oscar and had to return to America.'

'Did you win?' Chris asked.

'No, but the nomination meant I was never out of work.'

'Wow!' Chris said again. 'Imagine if *I* was nominated for an Oscar!'

Miss Snow laughed. 'You'd look very handsome in a suit for your acceptance speech.'

'And it would be presented by Jennifer Lawrence or Keira Knightley or Carey Mulligan or someone,' Chris said.

Jimmy giggled.

There was a sudden vibrating noise and Jimmy realised it was his mobile phone. Blushing furiously because he realised who it would be, he took it out of his pocket and answered it.

'JIMMY!'

'Hi, Mum, I'm just on my way home.'

'Are you, indeed?' Her voice was so loud that both Chris and Miss Snow could hear her.

'I'm only ten minutes away.'

'Ten minutes! Your tea is going to be burnt to a crisp. I don't know why I bother slaving away to feed you after a long day at work. It's not appreciated.'

Jimmy rolled his eyes and Miss Snow smiled sympathetically whilst Chris tried desperately to stop himself from laughing.

'I think I'd better go,' Jimmy said once he'd got rid of his mum.

'Well,' Miss Snow said as she saw them out, 'it's probably been about twenty years since I've been in the company of two such fine young men.'

Chris blushed to the very roots of his hair and Jimmy smiled.

'I've had a great time, Miss Snow,' Chris said.

'I hope we can do it again sometime,' she said. 'And I'll be seeing you again soon, won't I, Jimmy?'

'You can count on that.'

As they left, Jimmy turned to Chris. 'She's great, isn't she?'

Chris nodded. 'They don't make them like that anymore.'

As Jimmy and Chris walked back through the village towards the train station, they didn't notice Stoner and Wicks lurking behind the church wall opposite Penham Manor.

9. STONER'S STONES

When Jimmy woke up on Saturday morning, he realised that it was the Easter Holidays and that he didn't have anything to do for a whole three weeks. Except be an actor, of course. What an amazing idea, he thought. He had a job. Jimmy had never had a job before. As though getting a part in a West End play wasn't incredible enough, he was actually going to get paid for it too.

He got out of bed, took a shower and got dressed.

'You're up early,' his mum said, looking up from the sofa in their living room.

'Thought I might pop out.'

'Where?'

'A friend's.'

'Chris's?'

'Yeah,' Jimmy said.

'Take your mobile, won't you?'

Jimmy nodded. He was taking his mobile and his copy of the play for Miss Snow to look over.

There was a van outside Miss Snow's. *Whittaker's Windows.* And there was a man banging at the frame of one of the front windows from inside the house. Jimmy frowned and then strode up to the door and knocked. It was opened not by Miss Snow, but by a young girl.

'Who are you?' she asked.

Jimmy did a double take. It was the girl with vanilla hair. 'I'm Jimmy Catesby. I'm a friend of Miss Snow's.'

The girl stared at him as if he might be lying.

'Who is it, Sophia?' a woman's voice called from inside.

'A boy,' the girl said. 'You were at the theatre, weren't you?'

Jimmy nodded. 'I'm in the play.'

'So am I,' the girl said.

'Who are you?' Jimmy asked.

'That's a very rude question.'

'You asked me.'

'I'm Sophia,' the girl said. 'Sophia Snow. You'd better come in, hadn't you, if you're a friend of my grandmother's.'

Jimmy followed her into the front room where he saw the man at work on fixing a new window.

'Who's this?' A young woman, with shoulder-length hair the same colour as Sophia's, stared at Jimmy, a checked tea towel in her hand.

'He's a friend of grandmother's,' Sophia said.

'Is Miss Snow all right?' Jimmy asked, glancing round the living room.

'No,' the young woman said. 'Her window was broken by two youths.'

'What happened?'

'We're still trying to find out. It happened yesterday.'

Jimmy's mouth went dry. He had a nasty suspicion about who was responsible.

'Is she all right?'

The woman sighed. 'They left her alone – thank heavens – but she fell over trying to get to the telephone and there was an awful mess.'

'Is she in hospital?'

'Jimmy?' a faint voice called from upstairs. 'Is that my Jimmy?'

'Miss Snow!' Jimmy called back and, leaving the front room, bounded up the stairs two at a time.

'You can't go up there,' the woman yelled after him. 'She has to rest.'

But Jimmy was already at the top of the stairs. 'Miss Snow?'

'I'm in here, Jimmy.'

Jimmy opened a door and saw Miss Snow lying in a massive brass bed. She was sitting up in a nest of cosy white pillows with a fluffy duvet around her. She looked paler than he'd ever seen her and there were tears glistening in her eyes.

'What happened?'

'Oh, Jimmy,' she said as he walked forward and sat down on the bed next to her, the sweet smell of her lavender perfume wafting over him in a heavenly cloud. 'It was too awful. After you left the other day with your friend, I heard the most terrible sound of glass breaking. Somebody had thrown a rock through my window.'

'Were you hurt?'

'I suppose I could've been if I'd been asleep in my favourite chair, but I was in the kitchen.'

'You fell over?'

'Yes, silly me. I thought I'd try and get the police round to catch them, but I tripped and fell.'

'Are you all right?'

'I'm absolutely fine. A few bruises – that's all. My daughter – you met my daughter downstairs?'

Jimmy nodded.

'Catherine. She insists I stay in bed, but there's nothing wrong with me.'

'Did you see who threw the rock?'

'I only saw two youths running away through the

village.'

Jimmy bit his lip. He felt the same rage burning through him as he had when Stoner had pinned him to the ground. 'It's my fault, Miss Snow,' he said.

'What do you mean? How can it be your fault? Jimmy?'

He looked up at her. 'I got into a fight before I came here yesterday.'

'A fight? I can't believe that,' Miss Snow said. 'You don't fight, do you, Jimmy?'

He sighed. There was no hiding from her.

'You can tell me. It won't go any further.'

He swallowed, knowing she was telling the truth and deciding to do likewise himself. 'Two year ten boys – Stoner and Wicks – they don't like me. They think acting is weird.'

Miss Snow took this information in. 'I see. And so they pick on you, do they? Bully you?'

Jimmy nodded. 'Only Chris turned up and stopped them.' Jimmy smiled as he remembered. 'He was really amazing. He showed them.'

Miss Snow was frowning. 'I'm not sure I like the sound of that.'

'Oh, he didn't hurt them – not like they hurt me. He only warned them.'

'So they wanted to get their own back, did they? They followed you both, didn't they?'

'They must've done. I feel so stupid for not seeing them.'

'It's not your fault, Jimmy. You can't be held responsible for their behaviour.'

'But what are we going to do?'

'I don't think there's much we can do. There's no proof that it was this Stoner and Wicks.'

'But it *must* have been them,' Jimmy said in exasperation.

'I'm afraid that's not enough.'

Jimmy's face darkened with anger. 'It's so unfair. I wish I could show them. If I was stronger-'

'That's not the answer and you mustn't think it is. People like them always get their just desserts.'

'Do they?'

Miss Snow smiled. 'We have to hope they do. But we can't have this bullying continuing. Does your mum know?'

Jimmy shook his head. 'She'd just worry non-stop if she did or go to the school and make a big fuss and that would only make things worse.'

'But it can't go on.'

They sat for a few moments in silence. That was the strange thing about being with Miss Snow, Jimmy thought – he didn't feel under pressure to talk all the time. He was quite happy just to sit with her.

'I'm no good at doing nothing,' Miss Snow said and Jimmy nodded in agreement. 'I've read all my books, my eyes aren't good enough for sewing anymore and Catherine won't even let me go around the house with a duster and the place must be shrouded with dirt by now from that open window.'

Jimmy smiled. 'It looks fine to me.'

Miss Snow shook her head. 'I like the place looking spick and span.'

They were quiet again for a while and Jimmy could hear Catherine moving around downstairs, fussing over nothing.

'What do you think of my granddaughter?' Miss Snow asked with a smile as wide as her face.

'She's very nice,' he said honestly.

Jimmy was suddenly aware of another presence in the room and turned to see Sophia standing in the doorway.

'Ah, Sophia, this is one of my best friends, Jimmy.'

Jimmy smiled at hearing himself referred to in such honoured terms.

'We met at the theatre,' Sophia said.

'Of course,' Miss Snow said. 'But you're not to be in the same *family*, I understand.'

'No,' Sophia said.

Jimmy looked at her. She was very beautiful and yet he hadn't seen her smile. Jimmy wondered why. Perhaps she didn't like the look of him and was wondering what he was doing befriending her grandmother.

'You look too different, don't you?' Miss Snow said.

Jimmy turned. What did she mean? They looked too different to be friends? Was that why Sophia wasn't smiling at him? Did she think he looked odd?

'To be cast in the same family,' Miss Snow said, clearly seeing Jimmy's look of puzzlement. 'You're as dark as Sophia is fair.'

'Oh, yes,' Jimmy said. Why was he feeling so flustered all of a sudden? He looked at Miss Snow who was smiling lightly at the pair of them as if she was hiding a wonderful secret.

'How are you feeling, Grandma?'

'Just a little tired.'

'She's got a lot of bruises,' Sophia told Jimmy. 'I wish we could catch whoever it was who did this.' Her face was grim and Jimmy thought he could see tears swimming in her eyes and he knew then that something had to be done about Stoner and Wicks.

He knew he could do nothing on his own, but there was somebody who could help him.

Chris.

10. THE CASTING DIRECTOR

It was Monday morning and Jimmy's mum was just finishing breakfast when he entered the kitchen.

'You're up early. You haven't forgotten it's the holidays, have you?'

Jimmy shook his head. 'I like getting up early.'

'Since when?'

'Since recently.'

'It's news to me.'

'Don't want to waste the day,' Jimmy said.

'And what will you be doing today? You sure you'll be all right because I can easily drop you off at Isla's on the way to work.'

'I'll be fine, Mum,' Jimmy said quickly. He could think of nothing worse than being babysat by Isla. She was well-meaning and a great friend of his mum's, but she would insist on endless rounds of Scrabble or persuade Jimmy to watch the daytime chat shows with her as if he couldn't amuse himself. She'd even given him a pair of pink knitting needles once in the hope that he might take an interest.

'She always loves to see you and I feel better knowing you've got a bit of company.'

'But I'll not be on my own,' Jimmy said. 'I'll be with Chris most of the holiday,' Jimmy said honestly.

'When am I going to meet this Chris?'

Probably on opening night, Jimmy thought with an inward smile.

'Yeah, whenever,' Jimmy said.

His mum smiled at him across the cornflakes. 'Well, have a good day and don't be late home. I'm cooking something new. And keep your mobile on in case I need to get hold of you.'

Jimmy swallowed. He wasn't sure they'd be allowed to have mobile phones on during rehearsals. He'd just have to risk it.

At least he knew the way to the theatre once he was at Piccadilly. It felt strangely elating to be there again – as a real hired actor this time.

'Jimbo!' Chris called from the other side of the drama studio when he walked in. Jimmy waved and joined him on a long bench. Ben Farley, Amy and Diana were already in the room, standing talking together by the window. And then, everything became a blur of activity. They were divided into 'families' comprising of a mother, father, two brothers and a sister, and then spent the day reading through the script together and acting out scenes in pairs, finally coming together for another full reading at the end of the day. It was thoroughly exhausting, but wonderfully exhilarating. Jimmy felt his head would explode from so much concentration when the day finally came to an end, but he'd enjoyed every single minute.

He hadn't seen much of Sophia Snow. As she'd said at Miss Snow's, she was in a different 'family' group. The show had three families altogether which would take it in turn to perform on stage. However, the role of the mother and father would be played by only one actor and actress whereas three sets of children were needed for two-day stints. It was rather complicated.

'So, our 'parents' aren't really our parents,' Chris said.

'I think we've got the understudies,' Jimmy said.

'Who've the other group got, then?'

'More understudies? Maybe they've just been brought in for the rehearsals,' Jimmy said.

'Have you heard that Tim Versteegen is going to play the father?'

'Really? I haven't seen him here.'

'Apparently, he can't join rehearsals until next week. That's what I've heard,' Chris said, tapping his nose.

'That would be brilliant,' Jimmy said, suitably impressed. Tim Versteegen was a huge TV star. A George Clooney look-alike, he was currently a big hit in the BBC1 drama, *One Step at a Time.*

Chris said. 'Anyway, I gotta run.'

'Good – er – break a leg,' Jimmy said.

He was just about to leave himself when Ben Farley approached him.

'Good day, Jimmy?'

'Brilliant,' he said.

'We're very happy to have you on board,' Ben said, and then looked around him to see who was about. 'Listen, keep it quiet,' he said, 'but I've got this film project coming up and I think you should audition for the role of Michael. You'll need to see the casting director, Roberta Danes. I've got the details here. I've told her a bit about you and she'd love to see you.'

Jimmy took a crumpled piece of paper from Ben. It was a map with an address on.

'What do I have to do?'

'She'll give you some pieces to read. Can you go over now?'

Jimmy's eyes widened. It would mean being late back home. He would be risking the wrath of his mother after he'd promised to be at home on time for dinner – a dinner she was taking great care to prepare.

He took a deep breath and nodded. It was worth the risk.

'Oh, and Jimmy?' Ben said.

Jimmy turned back. 'Yes?'

'Don't let Roberta scare you.'

Jimmy got off the tube at South Kensington. He hadn't been sure what to expect. After an audition in a proper West End theatre, he'd expected something a bit more impressive than a private house. But it was a beautiful building: part of a long terrace of white house with railings outside and a flight of steps up to the front door. Jimmy climbed the steps and noticed that there was an intercom with two bells. *Dr PJ Dorchester.* Sounded like somebody you'd only visited when in extreme distress. *Ms R Danes.* That was the one he wanted. He pressed the bell and, a moment later, a dusty-sounding voice answered.

'Hello.'

'Hello. I'm James Catesby – I've come to audition.'

'Come up the stairs and bang on the red door,' the dusty voice said, 'and bring up any post.' Jimmy heard a buzzing sound and pushed open the front door. He found himself standing in a rather grand, but very dark hallway with a tiled floor and an old-fashioned hat stand on which were hung three old coats and a broken umbrella.

Post. She'd said something about post. Jimmy looked around. There was a pile on top of an empty bookcase at the bottom of the stairs. He examined the motley envelopes, selecting four that were addressed to: Roberta Danes, Ms Danes, RA Danes, and The Right Honourable Roberta Danes. Jimmy blinked. He had no idea what that meant, but it sounded awfully posh.

A steep staircase with an old red carpet led Jimmy up to the first floor where there was the promised red door on which was hung a notice: ROBERTA DANES – CASTING. AUDITION AT YOUR OWN RISK.

Jimmy gulped and then knocked on the door.

'Door's open,' the dusty voice called.

Jimmy stepped inside, finding himself in a bright red hall hung with mirrors of all different shapes and sizes.

'Come on through. I'm in the library.'

The library? Did apartments have libraries? Obviously this one did and Jimmy found it at the end of the hallway on the right and there, sitting behind a desk the size of a car, was a woman whom he guessed to be Roberta Danes.

'Did you say you were Aubrey Phipps or James Catesby?'

'James Catesby,' Jimmy said, thanking his lucky stars that he hadn't been lumbered with a name like Aubrey Phipps.

'Good lad. Phipps is out anyway. Nobody messes me around. He was meant to be here three days ago.'

Jimmy watched as she lit some sort of cigarette at the end of a very long filter. The room was dimly lit, but he could make out that she was very tall and thin in an elegant, dancer-like way, with brilliant black hair tumbling out of some sort of turban-style hat. It was impossible to tell how old she was, but her face was plastered with pink blusher and her eyes were shimmering with eye-shadow and mascara.

'I brought your post.'

'Good lad,' she said, taking it from him and perusing it with a wrinkled nose. 'Hateful bills. What shall I do with them?' But she already had her answer for they ended up on the floor next to a similar collection of envelopes. 'Now, what else are you going to give me?'

Jimmy looked puzzled for a moment. 'I don't have anything else.'

'Of course you have,' she said, waving her very long cigarette in the air. The dim room was thick with smoke; it was like some kind of indoor fog.

'No, really, I only brought your post.'

She laughed and she sounded far more like a man than a lady. 'Your performance, silly.'

'Oh! Ben – er – Mr Farley told me you'd give me something to read.'

'He did, did he? He is a pain.' Roberta Danes switched a lamp on and the room was thrown into semi-light and Jimmy noticed shelf upon shelf of books stretching from the floor to the ceiling.

'Wow!' he couldn't help saying.

'You like books?'

'I *love* books.'

'Me too,' she said, sucking on her filter until her cheekbones became as sharp as knife edges. 'They're constant companions. Far more faithful than people. They're always there: unchangeable and giving.'

Jimmy nodded. He agreed.

'Well,' Roberta said, squinting at the shelves, 'there must be something here you can read from. I'd give you one of those scripts,' she said, nodding towards her desk, 'but they're not really suitable. I can't see you in the role of an overweight fifty-year old.'

'I could give it a go,' Jimmy said gamely.

Roberta laughed like a man again.

'Or I could read some of my lines from *Family Matters* if you like.'

She looked at him. 'I would like,' she said, getting up from behind her desk to sit in a huge winged chair that was covered in clashing silk scarves of turquoise, magenta and scarlet.

'Could you read the part of Mark?' Jimmy asked.

'Do I look like a Mark to you?'

Jimmy swallowed. 'Sorry, I-'

'I'm only teasing. Give it to me.' She held out her hand and Jimmy handed over his copy of *Family Matters*, noticing her long nails painted a shocking orange. 'You don't need the play yourself?'

Jimmy wondered if she was testing him. 'No,' he said confidently. 'I know the part.'

Her eyebrows rose a fraction and she inhaled on her cigarette before beginning.

Jimmy had chosen the scene he'd rehearsed with Chris at the audition. He could do it in his sleep now.

Trying not to cough on the smoke-fog, Jimmy acted out the scene with Roberta doing a very good job in the role of Mark. Her voice was, Jimmy thought, probably deeper than Chris's. Once again, Jimmy had that marvellous experience of being wholly in another world and his heart was beating wildly when they finished.

Roberta Danes got up from the chair and put the script down on her desk and closed her eyes, displaying rainbow stripes of eye-shadow.

Jimmy waited for her to say something and began to worry when she didn't. Was she closing her eyes because she couldn't believe how awful he'd been?

'Ms Danes?' he asked at last in a faint whisper.

She opened her eyes. 'Ah, Jimmy,' she said, as if she'd completely forgotten he was there. Had his performance sent her to sleep?

'Would you like me to read again?'

'No, no, no,' she said, handing him the script back. 'That was quite enough.'

Jimmy blinked and watched. Oh, dear. What had he done? He thought it had gone okay, but it was very hard to judge your own performance.

'Do you want me to-'

'I'll be in touch,' she said, getting up and stretching out a long, orange-taloned hand which Jimmy shook.

'Thank you,' he said politely.

She didn't offer to show him out, but Jimmy was relieved. He wanted out of there as quickly as possible. He'd never felt so embarrassed in his life and, to top it all, he was going to be horribly late home now.

11. PROFESSOR NUTBERRY

His mum was waiting for him in the living room and she was wearing the kind of expression the Devil would have nightmares about.

'James Alexander Catesby!'

Jimmy almost swallowed his tongue. He must *really* be in trouble. He was used to being called James when his mum was a) angry with him or b) in a public place and wanting to sound posh, but *James Alexander*. That was bad.

He decided to try and intercept her anger with a heartfelt apology.

'Mum! I'm so sorry. I tried to call, but my phone died. I know I'm really late and I promise it won't happen again.'

'No, it *won't* happen again! If you're big enough to stay out at all hours, you're big enough to cook your own dinner.'

Wasn't she being just a little unfair? It was only ten past seven – not exactly the middle of the night. But it was forty minutes later than he'd promised and that forty minutes had obviously not done his dinner any good at all.

He followed her into the kitchen where she opened the oven door and a cloud of dark smoke wafted out.

'It looks fine, Mum,' Jimmy said.

She unceremoniously dumped what had once been a casserole onto the kitchen table.

'Ruined,' she said.

'No, it's not,' Jimmy said, helping himself to a large spoonful which he placed on his plate, trying not to wince at the dark vegetables which looked as if they'd fossilised.

'I told you I was cooking and you said you'd be home.'

'I'm sorry, Mum,' Jimmy said again. He should have known not to mess with his mother on a cooking night. Cooking nights were rare events in the Catesby household. They normally ate pizza, oven chips, mashed potato or things from the freezer covered in breadcrumbs. His mum wasn't a natural cook and, after a full day's work, she hardly ever felt inclined to actually prepare something homemade. 'It's good,' Jimmy said, forcing a dark mouthful down with a quick chase of water.

His mum watched him with suspicious eyes.

'Honest. Try some.'

'I've had mine,' she said, her voice distinctly cool.

Jimmy ate in silence for a while, doing his best with what lay on his plate. Each mouthful was a battle and his mother wasn't going to let him off the hook before he'd suffered. He sighed inwardly, betting his life that Tom Hanks had never had to eat such grisly offerings.

'Oh, for goodness' sake, Jimmy, leave it,' she said at last.

'But it's goo-'

'*Leave* it!'

Jimmy put his knife and fork down.

'Where exactly were you?'

Jimmy looked up. 'I told you, I was with Chris.'

His mum didn't look at all happy. 'Why don't I believe you, Jimmy?'

Jimmy didn't know what to say. He couldn't think of any smart reply and, even if he could, he wouldn't dared have said it with his mum in the mood she was in.

'Give me his number,' his mum said.

'Mum!'

'*Now*, James. I won't ask again.'

Jimmy was tempted to say, *Good*, and leg it out of the house, but he knew better than that so, reluctantly, he gave his mobile to his mum ready to dial Chris's number. He could only hope that Chris would back him up and not mention anything about London or the play.

'Hello. Is that Chris? This is Fiona Catesby – Jimmy's mum. Yes. That's right. I'm very well, thank you. Has he? Oh, well, I hope it's all nice things you've heard about me.'

Jimmy smiled. Chris was charming her already.

'Really?' His mum laughed. She was blushing. Chris was making her blush. 'That's very sweet of you to say so. Listen, Chris-'

Jimmy swallowed. He could only sweet-talk her for so long.

'Was Jimmy with you today?'

There was a pause which seemed to last a lifetime.

'He was? Okay. Well, do you mind me asking where you live?'

Jimmy held his breath. Please, *please* don't say Camden, he begged silently.

'LONDON!' his mother suddenly shouted. 'What do you mean, *London?*'

Jimmy almost leapt out of his seat. What was Chris telling her?

'What?' she said. 'I don't understand.'

Again, there was a long pause and Jimmy waited, sure that he was going to break into a sweat at any moment.

'Really? No, he hasn't mentioned it.'

Jimmy watched his mum's face, trying to fathom what was being said at the other end of the phone.

'Well, Chris,' his mum said at last, 'thank you for being so honest with me. No, that's quite all right. I understand. And I'd very much like to meet you too one day,' she said and hung up before turning to Jimmy, her expression slightly softer than before. 'Why didn't you tell me?'

Jimmy's eyes widened. He didn't dare say anything for fear of landing himself in it.

'You should have said something, sweetheart.'

Sweetheart? This was becoming more and more confusing by the minute.

'I know you've always struggled with maths. In fact, I should've thought of it for you. I'm such a bad mother. But extra lessons during your holiday. What a great idea. It'll all be worthwhile too, I'm sure. I'm so proud of you. And a professor too. What's he like? And you must tell me what the university is like. I've never been to a real university before.'

Jimmy gulped. Was this for real? What had got into Chris? Extra maths lessons – at a London university – with a professor?

'I didn't know if you'd agree,'

'Of course I'd agree,' his mum said. 'It's for your education and there's nothing more important than that, is there? And this Professor Nutberry is one of the best teachers in the country, Chris said.'

Professor Nutberry! Jimmy did his best not to break into a fit of laughter. 'Yes,' Jimmy said, deciding it was best to get into the swing of things. 'He is. He's amazing. He makes everything seem so simple. I'm actually enjoying algebra,' Jimmy said, and then suddenly wondered where that sentence had come from. What a weird thing for him to say.

'And what's the university like?'

Jimmy's mind raced. 'Big,' he said, deciding that was a safe bet. 'You wouldn't believe how big it is. I got lost going to the toilet.'

His mum laughed.

'And the classrooms are really cool – not like the scruffy ones at school. And there are computers everywhere – even in the toilets.'

'The toilets?' His mum's forehead wrinkled in surprise.

Jimmy bit his tongue. What had made him say that? 'Yeah,' he said, 'little ones with timetables on so everyone knows what lessons are on and where they are.'

'Well I never!'

Jimmy thought he'd better shut up before he said something really outrageous.

His mum got up from the table and grabbed her handbag from a worktop, opening it and taking a twenty pound note out of her purse. 'You should have told me, Jimmy. How have you been paying your train fare?'

'I've got a bit put by.'

His mother sighed. 'That's your savings. Here.' She handed him the money and Jimmy felt terribly guilty about taking it. He realised that now was the time to tell her what he was really up to. She'd be furious with him, of course, but it was bound to be far worse if he left it until later.

'Mum.'

'Yes.'

'I have to –' he paused.

'What?' His mum smiled at him. She was in a good mood, but that could change so quickly.

'I have to get on with the – er – homework.'

'He sets you homework?'

'Of course,' Jimmy said, getting up from the table. 'He is a professor, Mum.'

'Chris!' Jimmy yelled across the studio when he arrived at rehearsals the next day.

'Hey, Jimbo!'

'What on earth was that story you told my mum?'

'Your old lady's okay,' Chris said, a big grin plastered on his face. 'What? Didn't you like my university story?'

'I thought it was a stroke of genius,' Jimmy said, sitting down on the bench next to him. 'Trouble is, my mum's really bought into the idea and if my maths doesn't start to improve for real, I'll be in a right mess.'

'But she'll know about the play before then, won't she? You're going to have to tell her.'

Jimmy shook his head.

'I don't get it. Won't she be proud?'

'She's not really into the idea of me wanting to be an actor. She says it's too unstable and there's never enough work.'

'I suppose she'd rather you do a safe, boring job.'

Jimmy nodded. 'Hey, how did your pizza job go?'

'I got it,' Chris said. 'Means I don't have to work in that rat-hole fast food joint anymore. But don't go telling my brother or he'll put my rent up.'

Another day of rehearsals began. Jimmy was well ahead of the other cast members in that he could almost run through the entire play without reference to his script. Chris was pretty good too.

'The effortless memory of youth,' said Julia, the lady who was understudying the part of the mother.

In the afternoon Ben had a special treat for them, leading them along the corridor to the stage. Jimmy had never been backstage before and was fascinated by the endless ropes, lights and set pieces that were there. The props for the play hadn't arrived yet nor had the costumes, but he couldn't wait to see everything in place.

Ben led the way out onto the bare stage and Jimmy gasped as he looked out into the auditorium at row upon row of empty seats. It was quite spooky to imagine that this was the stage he'd be performing on and that each of these seats – if the play sold well – would be filled. Each person in each of those seats would be watching him.

'Blimey,' Chris said under his breath. 'This is something else.'

Jimmy looked up at the ornate gold-painted plasterwork around the boxes and wondered if his mum and Miss Snow would book one of those. Or would they sit in the front row? Or would his mum not come at all? No, no. He wasn't going to have negative thoughts now.

He gazed up at the incredible chandelier positioned high above the auditorium. Everything was so beautiful in the theatre. It was easy to see why people came: it was an escape from the ugliness and reality of ordinary life. That's what being an actor was all about, Jimmy thought – helping people to escape.

'What do you think?' Ben asked and everyone answered at once:

'Wow!'

'It's amazing.'

'Scary!'

'It's so beautiful.'

'I love it.'

'Wait till you see it dressed for the play. We'll be able to rehearse out here soon. But, meanwhile, it's back to the studio.'

Jimmy didn't want to leave the stage. He was well and truly smitten. He could quite happily have moved the contents of his bedroom there and set up home.

He was the last to leave the stage and Ben was waiting for him in the wings.

'I had a phone call from Roberta Danes last night,' Ben said.

Jimmy grimaced. He'd conveniently managed to forget about that experience.

'She was very impressed, Jimmy.'

'She was?'

Ben nodded. 'You must have worked your charm on the old girl.'

'But she hardly spoke to me. I thought she hated me.'

Ben laughed. 'That's just her way. But she wants to put you forward for the role of Michael. The director will have to approve, of course.'

'What's the director like?' Jimmy asked, knowing that Ben was involved in the film.

'I'm afraid he's very tough,' Ben said. 'I've always said I wouldn't work with him again.'

Jimmy sighed, but Ben was smiling. Jimmy narrowed his eyes. 'It's you, isn't it?'

Ben laughed again and nodded. 'I'm sorry I put you through the ordeal of meeting Roberta, but she likes to see all the new talent and pricked her ears up when I mentioned you. She also knows everything that's going on in the business so you never know.'

You never know. Jimmy liked those words. They were full of promise and spoke of tomorrow.

They spent the rest of the afternoon improvising scenes based on those in the play. It was a good, fun way of learning about the characters whilst not stressing about lines.

Chris and Jimmy left the theatre together.

'Some day, huh? Guess you'll have to come up with some mathematical story to tell your mum.'

Jimmy rolled his eyes. 'Do you think I should buy a book or something to make things look more real?'

'Wouldn't do any harm.'

They walked back towards the tube together.

'Chris,' Jimmy said, suddenly remembering Miss Snow. He quickly told Chris exactly what had happened to her after they'd left Penham Manor.

'Why didn't you tell me before?'

'I forgot,' Jimmy said. He felt terrible. How could he have forgotten about Miss Snow lying in bed covered in bruises? He'd been so wrapped up in the rehearsals and the excitement of Ben sending him to audition for a casting agent that he'd completely forgotten what should have been his number one priority.

'I can't believe they followed us,' Chris said. His eyes were dark with fury. 'Not after I warned them.'

Chris, Jimmy suspected, wasn't used to having people testing his patience.

'What are we going to do?' Jimmy asked.

Chris stopped walking for a moment and stared at a filthy patch of London pavement. 'Plenty,' he said at last. 'We're going to do plenty.'

12. REVENGE

Jimmy was watching *Rear Window* in the front room and was just wondering what it must have been like to kiss Grace Kelly when his mum came in.

'I've just had Isla on the phone,' she said.

Jimmy looked up, reluctantly, from the television. He hated being interrupted when in film mode, but his mum's voice sounded funny.

'Apparently,' she continued, 'two houses on the estate have had their windows smashed this evening.'

Jimmy's heart skipped a beat. 'What?'

'That's what I said.'

'Which ones?' Jimmy already knew the answer, but felt he needed it confirmed.

'Marjorie Wicks' and Bob Stoner's. Don't their sons go to your school?'

Jimmy nodded.

'Who on earth could have done such a thing? Mindless vandalism,' his mum said, shaking her head. 'Who would ever have thought it in Penham?'

'It happened up at Penham Manor earlier this week.'

'Did it? Must be the same person,' his mum said. 'Well, I hope it doesn't get any closer. You don't feel safe inside your own home anymore.'

Jimmy switched the television off and went upstairs. Closing his bedroom door, he reached for his mobile phone.

'Chris?'

'Jimbo?'

'Where are you?'

'I guess you already know if you're calling.'

'Why didn't you tell me?'

'Because you'd only have tried to talk me out of it. Am I right?'

'Of course you're right,' Jimmy said, thinking that Chris sounded out of breath as if he was running. 'Are you still in Penham?'

'Sure. I wanted to be around and see what happened.'

'Are you mad? What if the police turn up?'

'They've been and gone already – useless lot.'

'Chris, you're completely insane.'

'So I've been told.'

Jimmy frowned. He really was beginning to think that Chris wasn't all there.

'What on earth made you do it?' Jimmy asked.

'What do you mean? Are you saying I shouldn't have done it? I don't understand you, Jimbo. You asked me what we should do, didn't you?'

'I didn't mean-'

'What *did* you mean, then? I did what I thought was right. Like for like. An eye for an eye.'

'That's just plain dangerous. You know Stoner and Wicks will think it's us.'

'They'd be thicker than they look if they didn't.'

'So that lands us in even more trouble.'

Chris sighed. 'Don't you have any faith in me, little bro?'

'Not at the moment, no,' Jimmy confessed.

'Don't panic. I've got it all sorted,' Chris said and then he hung up.

Jimmy stared at his phone, his eyes glazed with pure fear because he knew who was going to suffer for this.

Don't panic, little bro, Chris had said. But it was all

right for him. Stoner and Wicks weren't likely to come after him, were they?

Jimmy didn't enjoy rehearsals the next day as much as he should have. His mind was on other things. Chris didn't seem at all bothered. He was completely focussed on his role as Mark Tranter. Jimmy wished he could be more relaxed, but his stomach was churning at the thought of going home.

Chris travelled with him on the tube, but they didn't speak much. Jimmy looked out of the window as the city melted away behind them and the countryside began. Flats became terraces and then semis and, finally, pretty rows of cottages.

They got off at Penham Station and Chris turned to Jimmy.

'So, you know what to do?' he said and Jimmy nodded, watching as Chris legged it out of the station before Jimmy had a chance to say anything. Swallowing hard, he left the station himself and took the path that led to the village. This, he thought, was worse than any audition. His heart was pounding and his head felt thick.

The village was quiet. An old man rode by on a bike and a young couple were getting into a car after having walked their dog. There was nobody else around and yet Jimmy knew instinctively that he wasn't alone.

He tried to think of something else. The stage. How beautiful it was. How incredible it was going to be to perform there. Think. *Think!* But it was no good. Jimmy was routed firmly in the present. There was no getting away from it. It was going to happen and he just had to get through it.

'THERE HE IS!' Stoner's voice suddenly shouted from one of the footpaths at the side of a cottage and Jimmy felt the familiar rush of fear.

He didn't need to be told what to do: he ran. He ran faster than he'd ever done before – faster than any sports day because, if he didn't, he would fail. He had to make it. If he could just make it to the church.

His adrenalin rush seemed to fuel him and he sped through the village – the shops and houses blurring past him – his mind focussed on one thing only.

'CATESBY!' Stoner called, his feet pounding on the road behind Jimmy. But Jimmy didn't dare to look back because it would slow him down. On he went, his feet fast and furious. Just a bit further, he told himself. He was almost there…

SPLAT!

For a moment, the world stopped. Jimmy was on the ground. How had that happened?

He felt dizzy.

Get up. Get up! a voice inside told him, but he couldn't move at first.

'TIGHTS BOY!'

They're catching up, the voice said and, heaving himself onto all fours, he struggled to his feet and started running again. He was nearly there – nearly at the church. He could feel himself slowing down and he allowed himself a glance behind him.

Stoner was just behind him now and Wicks wasn't far behind Stoner. Jimmy felt the familiar hands grab his shoulders and he was on the ground again.

'You little IDIOT!' Stoner spat in his ear as he pushed him with an angry fist. 'It was you, wasn't it?'

'What?'

'The windoz. You broke 'em.'

'What windows? I don't know what you're talking about.'

'Don't get smart with me, Tights Boy. Who else could it 'ave bin?'

Wicks hovered over him, an ugly grin on his face. 'Unless it was that moron big brother of yours.'

'Was it 'im?' Stoner probed, getting hold of Jimmy's arm behind his back and twisting it until Jimmy yelled.

'Yes!'

'What?'

'It was him.'

Stoner let go of Jimmy for a minute and spat on the ground beside him. 'You'd better tell 'im he's in big trouble.'

'Why don't you tell me yourself?' Chris said, suddenly appearing from behind the church wall.

For a brief moment, Stoner looked lost.

'I broke your windows because you broke Mary Snow's, didn't you?'

'Yeah? So what? What business is it of yours?'

'I'm making it my business, okay? That's all you need to know,' Chris said, walking forward. 'And I thought I'd told you to lay off the bullying. How many times have you bullied Jimmy and the others from school?'

'They deserve everything they get.'

'Says who?'

'Sez me,' Stoner said, his eyes narrowing as if he was willing up the strength to attack Chris at any moment.

'Well I say it's going to stop.'

Stoner and Wicks gave an incredulous laugh. 'Yeah? You reckon?'

'I do,' Chris said calmly as he helped Jimmy up. 'Because I've got proof of what you did.'

'What're you talkin' about?'

Chris calmly walked back to the wall of the church and picked up a tiny camera which had been resting, unseen, capturing everything. 'I've got everything on here,' he said, a triumphant grin on his face. 'Your confession to breaking the window, to bullying, picking on Jimmy-'

'Why you-' Stoner made a move towards Chris. Quick as a flash, Chris placed the camera on the church wall and tackled Stoner to the ground until he yelled in pain. Wicks didn't dare come to his aid nor did he even think about retrieving the camera and, all the time, Jimmy watched in wonder.

'Did you want to say something?' Chris asked Stoner whose face was pressed against the ground. He looked like roadkill. 'Eh?'

Stoner didn't reply.

'I can't hear you,' Chris said in sing-song fashion, clearly enjoying the moment.

Still Stoner didn't reply.

'He's not got any manners, has he?' Chris said, forcing a knee into Stoner's back and twisting his arm as Stoner had done to Jimmy just minutes before. 'I take it we're not going to have any more trouble from you again.'

They waited for his answer. Stoner shook his head, his surly lips scraping against the road as he did so.

'Good,' Chris said, getting up and wiping his trousers down. 'I suggest you go home, then. No point hanging round here, is there?'

Stoner got up. His eyes looked murderous, but there was something of defeat in his posture. 'You're an idiot,' he told Chris. 'You show that tape to anyone and you're in fer it too.'

Wicks looked at Stoner and then at Chris. 'Yeah,' he said after having been mute for so long. 'They'll know you broke our windows.'

Chris laughed. 'I don't care,' he said, shrugging. 'You want to try me, eh? You want to see if I care. I don't give a damn if anyone knows what I did because I know it was the right thing to do.'

Stoner stared at him, seeming to wonder if Chris was bluffing. Was it worth finding out and risking his own neck?

He finally turned away and slunk back towards the village with a baffled Wicks following. There were no more threats, no protests – they just kept walking until they were out of sight.

Jimmy breathed a huge sigh of relief. 'Am I glad that's over.'

Chris shook his head. 'Blimey, for a minute back there, I didn't think we were going to pull it off.'

'YOU didn't think we were going to pull it off. I didn't think I was going to make it to the church. Thought they had me back in the village. Did you see me fall?'

'Did I? I nearly got up to help.'

Jimmy laughed. 'That would've ruined everything.'

Chris retrieved the camera from the church wall.

'Did you really film it all?'

'Oh, yes,' Chris said, rewinding it back and playing a bit at random. 'Do you think Miss Snow would like to see it?'

Jimmy looked up at the manor. Miss Snow's bedroom curtains were closed and there was a car out the front. 'I think her daughter's still there.'

'Maybe another time, then.'

They headed back through the village together. A strange peace flooded Jimmy. He could hardly believe it. He felt quite sure that that was the end of the Stoner and Wicks business. They wouldn't try anything else, would they? At least, not in Penham. They wouldn't dare. And, with that worry gone, all Jimmy had to fret about was when he was going to tell his mum about *Family Matters*.

13. FEARS AND DOUBTS

Life for Jimmy seemed to reach some level of normality after the Stoner and Wicks 'Caught on Camera' incident. Chris never referred to it again and they both threw themselves into rehearsals with great gusto.

The Easter holidays rushed by and, because Jimmy's mum thought he was going back to school, she stopped giving him his tube fare into town and he had to start eating into his savings again.

'Won't your maths teacher be surprised when you show him how much you've improved over the holidays,' Jimmy's mum said as she was getting ready for work.

Jimmy nodded, thinking of the lessons he was going to have to skip and how far behind he was going to get.

'Will you take that book in and show him?'

Jimmy had bought a very expensive maths book during one of his lunch times whilst at rehearsals and, whenever his mum had come into his bedroom during the evenings of the holiday, he made sure his eyes were fixed on some dastardly equation or a piece of unfathomable algebra.

'I don't know, Mum. If I take the book in, it might look as if I'm showing off.'

Jimmy's mum nodded. 'Well, I'm dead proud of you.' She leaned forward and kissed his cheek.

Jimmy felt so guilty. Would she be as proud of him when he confessed what he'd really been up to?

She would make you pull out, his inner voice told him. He remembered the time she'd caught him with one of her cigarettes. He hadn't been going to smoke it. He was pretending to be a detective from one of the old film noir movies he loved so much, but his mum had been so furious that he sincerely thought she'd have been less angry if he'd actually been smoking.

'I don't understand it. You're too old to be playing pretend,' she yelled at him.

But he wasn't playing pretend. He was *acting*. And he'd never be too old because he didn't ever want to stop. It was the only time he truly felt alive and he felt incredibly sad that his mum would never understand that. So he had to keep things covered up for as long as possible. Once the opening of the play was in sight, then he'd tell her because it would be too late then. She wouldn't stop him once she knew he was going to perform on a stage in the West End.

The only problem was getting time off school. The rehearsals were lasting longer than he'd thought. It wouldn't be so bad once the play was up and running as they had three sets of children and there would only be the occasional Wednesday matinee when he'd have to skip school. The evening performances would allow him plenty of time to get there from school and, by then, he'd have told his mum and so wouldn't have to lie about where he was going in the evenings. Not that she'd let him stay out until after ten at night and catch the train home by himself. But he was quite confident that he'd work that out when the time came.

In the meantime, he'd knuckle down to rehearsals and work on a convincing sick note to send to his form tutor, Mrs Huddlestone. He was getting pretty good at forging notes, he thought, thinking of the release note he'd forged and given to Ben Farley.

'No, Jimmy!' Ben hollered. 'The line's more subtle than that. It mustn't be shouted. Try it again.'

Jimmy took a deep breath. 'I think you've got him all wrong, Mum. He isn't like that-'

'NO!' Ben shouted, causing everyone in the studio to turn around. 'Jimmy, what's got into you?'

Jimmy stared at Ben, wide-eyed. 'I thought-'

'You're still yelling.'

Jimmy wanted to say that it was Ben who was doing all the yelling.

'I thought we'd got this scene sorted,' Ben said, scratching his head as if he had a very bad case of nits. Jimmy had never seen him so worked up before. Ben was usually Mr Laid-back and together, and Jimmy hated to think that he was the cause of it.

'Don't worry,' Grace said. She was playing the part of the mother and had worked with Ben before. 'He's always like this in the run-up to opening. He finds somebody to pick on and then takes all his frustrations out on them. Pity it's you, sweetheart.'

Jimmy shrugged his shoulders as if it didn't matter, but it was no comfort at all. In fact, he was beginning to wonder if the acting lark was such a good idea after all and whether he should jack it in and go back to school and the safety of a double maths lesson.

He was hoping things would calm down after lunch but, if anything, they seemed to get worse.

'No, no, NO!' Ben shouted. 'Are you even listening to me, Jimmy?'

Jimmy frowned. 'I'm listening.'

'I don't think you are. I've never seen you show such a lack of conviction. Who are you? Because you're not Philip Tranter at the moment and that's what I need.'

Jimmy really didn't know how to respond because he'd never been in a situation like this before. Miss Parnaby at school had never shouted at him like that. Come to think of it, neither had his own mother – not as badly as this, anyway. In fact, Jimmy half-expected Ben to yell, 'James Alexander Catesby!' across the studio in a bad imitation of his mother. Instead, he fixed Jimmy with a look of utter despair as if he was solely responsible for all the ills of the world.

'You think he's testing me?' Jimmy asked Chris when they stopped for a ten-minute break.

Chris was totally aghast. 'He's completely out of order, man,' he said. 'You want me to say something?'

'NO!' Jimmy said, worried in case Chris showed Ben the same sort of mercy that he'd shown Stoner and Wicks. 'Maybe I haven't got what it takes,' Jimmy said.

'Are you kidding? You're great. You're not going to let him get to you, are you? You've come this far already.'

Jimmy fixed his gaze on the floor. 'Maybe this is as far as it goes for me.'

Chris tutted and punched Jimmy on the shoulder. 'I don't know what's got into him today, but he sure is acting like a madman.'

But what if it wasn't just Ben having a bad day? What if there really was something wrong with Jimmy's acting and he wasn't able to make the grade? It was Ben who would bear the brunt of it for casting an unknown, and what if Jimmy showed him up in the real play? It would be a disaster and he'd never live it down. Maybe it was better if he bowed out now before it was too late. Or, he thought miserably, before Ben fired him.

As Jimmy took the train home, he felt as if all of his confidence had slid away in the space of one short day. He still couldn't think what had gone wrong. He didn't feel that his performance had been wildly different from any of the other rehearsals. If anything, he thought he was getting stronger as an actor. He'd felt far more sure of what he was doing. He felt less like a novice and more like a real actor and yet Ben had singled him out for criticism.

Later that evening, after doing some fake homework – he'd been writing in a notebook about what a terrible day he'd had – he went downstairs. His mum was sitting in her favourite chair with a mug of tea resting on the arm. She was flipping through a tatty magazine she'd obviously brought home from work.

'Mum?' he said.

'Yes?'

He sat on the sofa opposite and puffed out his cheeks like he did when he was building up to asking something important. 'Have you ever wanted to do something that was really important to you, but just couldn't do it?'

His mum looked at him. 'But I thought your maths was improving since Professor Nutberry-'

'I'm not talking about maths, Mum.'

'What then?'

He sighed. 'Doesn't matter.'

She got up to sit on the sofa next to him, ruffling his hair. 'What is it? What's bothering you?'

'Have you, Mum? Ever wanted something really badly, but weren't good enough to get it?'

His mum frowned and seemed to drift silently away into her past. 'Yes. But I suppose everybody has. It's not always easy getting what you want.'

'What did you want, Mum?'

Her eyes widened. 'Well, in the days before I was your mum,' she laughed, 'that seems so long ago now, but I guess I wanted to be a ballerina.'

'Did you?' It was the first Jimmy had heard about it.

'Of course. Every girl wants to be a ballerina. Like every boy wants to be a footballer.'

'I don't.'

'That's because you're different.' She gave his shoulder a squeeze.

'What stopped you from being a ballerina?'

'Oh, I don't know.' She puffed her cheeks out in just the way that Jimmy did. 'I suppose real life got in the way. You know. You get a job and a house. You get pregnant.'

'It wasn't me that stopped you doing what you wanted, was it?' Jimmy asked in horror.

'Of course not. I guess I just didn't want it enough.'

So, was that it, Jimmy wondered? Did you have to want something so badly that nothing would stop you from getting it? He thought of how hurt he'd felt when Ben had shouted at him from across the studio, and how humiliated he'd felt when everybody had turned to look at him. Was that what he had to overcome? Was it worth it?

Just how badly did Jimmy want to be an actor?

14. STAGE SCHOOL

Jimmy didn't go into the theatre the next morning. Nor did he go to school. He went to Miss Snow's.

It was strange walking through Penham in the middle of the morning. The village looked so pretty in the spring sunshine and there were people out shopping, walking dogs, and passing the time of day with neighbours. Jimmy walked on towards Penham Manor, looking at his watch and wondering if his absence at the theatre had been noticed yet.

The door was answered by Miss Snow's daughter, Catherine, who glared at Jimmy through narrowed eyes.

'Shouldn't you be at school?' she asked.

'No,' Jimmy said. 'I should be at rehearsals.'

She frowned, obviously thinking he was being cheeky.

'Jimmy?' Miss Snow's voice floated through from the front room and Catherine was forced to let him in.

'Miss Snow. How are you?' She was sitting in her favourite winged chair by the front window – the chair which had been showered with glass a few days before.

'I'm very well, Jimmy. All the better for seeing you. But what are you doing here?'

Jimmy gave a hopeless smile. 'I didn't-' he paused, 'that is, I-'

He turned to see Catherine Snow hovering behind him, impatient hands resting on impatient hips.

'Catherine, dear. Be a love and do that shop you promised me.'

'Now?'

'Yes,' Miss Snow said gently.

Catherine sighed. 'Very well, then.'

Once she'd left the house, Miss Snow said, 'Now, pull up that chair and tell me what's wrong.'

Jimmy did as he was told; he always did with Miss Snow. Looking across at the old lady, he noticed that her cheeks were a little less pale than they had been the last time he'd seen her and he was relieved to see her looking so much better.

'I'm not sure what to do,' he said in a very quiet voice.

'About what? What's happened?'

Jimmy gave a great sigh. 'I don't know if I can do it. I thought I could, but I'm not sure now.'

Miss Snow frowned. 'Do what? What are you talking about?'

'Act. I don't know if I can act.'

Miss Snow's bright face crinkled in utter bewilderment. 'Of *course* you can act. What's making you talk like this? Is it those bullies?'

'No,' Jimmy said. 'Chris has seen to it that they never bother anyone again.'

'Has he?'

Jimmy nodded. 'It was all above board,' he added quickly, lest Miss Snow should think that he and Chris were no better than bullies themselves.

'Well that's good news, but what's all this nonsense about not being able to act?'

'It's not nonsense. Ben told me.'

'Ben? No, Jimmy, you must've misunderstood. Ben wouldn't say-'

'He was shouting at me all day yesterday. Said I wasn't showing any conviction and that I was yelling my lines. Everybody was staring at me. It was awful. I felt so embarrassed.'

Miss Snow listened in silence as Jimmy got it all out of his system.

'Miss Parnaby's never shouted at me. She's always praising me and telling me how good I am. And I thought I was doing all right yesterday. I'd learned my lines which is more than some members of the cast. I thought it was going so well.' He paused.

'Is that all?'

Jimmy stared. 'What do you mean? Isn't that bad enough?'

Miss Snow chuckled. 'Your pride's been knocked a little – that's all. It's not in Ben's interests to praise you all the time. That's not a director's job. It's his job to get the best performance he can out of you. Acting's tough and you'll have to get used to being shouted at.'

'Then why wasn't he shouting at everybody else?'

'Maybe it was your turn to be shouted at? I bet he's having a good go at Chris today.'

Jimmy wasn't completely convinced by what Miss Snow had to say.

'Look,' she continued, 'it's like any other profession – there are good days and bad days. Nothing comes together without a little bit of work. Think of Ben like one of your school teachers if that helps. He might be a terrible bore – always yelling and shouting – but it's because he wants the very best from you.'

'It didn't feel like that yesterday. I felt I was being picked on.'

Miss Snow looked at him, her eyes full of sympathy. 'It's a tough profession,' she said. 'You've got to have skin like a suit of armour to withstand all the knocks.'

The phone rang. Miss Snow got up slowly and walked across the room to answer it.

'Well I never,' she said. 'We were just talking about you.'

Jimmy started. Was it Ben? Had he somehow – through some strange telepathy – heard what Jimmy had been saying about him and was ringing up to fire him?

'Yes, he's here, Ben. Do you want to talk to him?' Miss Snow looked across the room at Jimmy, but he shook his head. She beckoned to him and Jimmy reluctantly got up and took the receiver from her.

'Hello,' he said.

'Jimmy? It's Ben. I've been worried sick about you. Why aren't you here?'

'I didn't think-'

'I hope this doesn't have anything to do with yesterday, does it? Because I may have been a bit strong with the old comments. Is that it? Have I put you off? I hope I haven't, Jimmy, because you're one of the best I've seen in a long time. I think you can stay the course and make it. But I tend to get a bit worked up when I find a good actor. I want the very best from them. Do you understand? I have to push them. I have to get the best possible performance out of them and I'm never satisfied until I've done that.'

Jimmy listened, not quite believing what he was hearing. It was just as Miss Snow had predicted.

'Jimmy?'

'Yes.'

'Will you come back? I've had one of the understudies in your role this morning and, between you and me, he sucks.'

Jimmy couldn't help but laugh.

'Will you come and rescue us all?'

Jimmy bit his lip.

'I promise not to shout at you again,' Ben said. 'Well, actually, I don't, but at least you know now that it's nothing personal.'

There was a pause when they were both waiting for the other to say something.

'Okay,' Jimmy said at last. 'I'll come in.'

'That's great,' Ben said. 'I'll see you soon then?' And he hung up.

Jimmy looked across the room at Miss Snow who had a huge smile on her face. 'Everything okay, then?'

Jimmy grinned. 'I think so.'

'Jimmy?' Ben beckoned him over. It was five o'clock and Jimmy had been back at the studio since one o'clock. It had seemed strange at first and he'd felt rather self-conscious swanning in so late, but everybody had seemed pleased to see him.

'Jimmy!' Grace had hollered across the studio.

'Jimbo!' Chris had bellowed.

And there was Ben, smiling and waving for Jimmy to join back in where he belonged. Now, he was calling him over again and Jimmy only hoped it wasn't to tell him that there'd been some terrible mistake and that Jimmy was now out and the understudy would be taking his role. He was still feeling so insecure about everything. But Ben didn't look as if he was about to fire him.

'A little bird told me that you might be interested in applying for a post at a drama school,' Ben said.

Jimmy nodded, wondering if the little bird was

Chris or Miss Snow.

'I've been in touch with some friends of mine. They run *The West London Stage School.* They've sent me an application form for a scholarship place.'

'Really?' Jimmy took the form from Ben.

'It's tough applying for a place in year 8. It's a very small school and most students start in year 6 and hold onto their places so there aren't many that become available. But why not try, eh?' he said, patting him on the back. 'Fill it in and take it round before the end of this week. I'll let you out early tomorrow so you can go and get a look at the place. See what you think.'

Jimmy looked at the form. *The West London Stage School.* It was the stuff his dreams were made of.

True to his word, Ben let Jimmy out early the next day and he hopped on the tube, travelling the short distance to the school. A huge bubble of excitement was lodged in his stomach at the thought of actually going into the building. He'd only recently found out that there were such things as drama schools. He'd discovered that there were several excellent ones in London and all boasted stars of film, TV and stage amongst their graduating pupils. They were expensive and competitive, but Jimmy couldn't think of a place he'd rather be. Imagine a school that trained you to become an actor. He couldn't wait to tell Miss Parnaby about it. Perhaps she'd been to one herself and she'd be able to give him some tips. As it was, Jimmy only had an application form and a letter of reference from Ben.

'Be sure and take this with you,' he'd said just before Jimmy had left. It was incredibly generous of

Ben seeing as he'd only known Jimmy for a few short weeks, but Jimmy guessed that he needed all the help he could get and he couldn't imagine his form tutor, Mrs Huddlestone, writing a glowing reference for him. Not with his track record and the way she was always shouting at him. No, Mrs Huddlestone would definitely be an *anti*-referee if there was such a thing. Jimmy grinned. Perhaps there was. They'd be the people you'd put down if you *didn't* want to get a job – if you'd been forced into applying for something that your heart really wasn't in like if Jimmy's mum pushed him into getting a job in her office when he left school. He could put Mrs Huddlestone down as his referee, get rejected and say to his mum, 'Oh, no! I really don't know what happened.'

But he had Ben Farley as a referee. That was incredible and, seeing as he hadn't stuck the envelope down on his letter of reference, Jimmy nipped into a newsagents and got half a dozen copies just in case he needed one in the future. Reading it on the tube, his heart swelled with pride, his eyes skipping over the most wonderful phrases again and again:

… a rare talent … approaches tasks with energy and enthusiasm … ability to learn a play quickly and with profound insight … I heartily recommend him as I'm sure he will make an exemplary student.

The West London Stage School was on a quiet backstreet lined with smart Victorian terraces; the school itself was housed in a large red-brick building with huge glass windows and an arched door with a flight of steps leading up to it. Jimmy gave a low whistle. It was certainly more imposing than the concrete monstrosity that was Penham High.

He crossed the road and entered. There was a sign to reception, but Jimmy got a bit sidetracked by the corridors. They weren't like Penham High's corridors full of ancient pupils' work that was half-fallen, half-torn from the walls. These corridors were lined with framed photographs in which students were smiling. There were pupils on stage taking curtain calls, pupils being made up in dressing rooms, pupils in costumes receiving prizes. Everybody looked so happy because everybody was doing exactly what they wanted to be doing. It was a complete revelation to Jimmy that school could be such a place. To him, school meant drudgery: death by decimals, boredom through biology and frustration in French, but these pupils made school look like a holiday camp.

Walking down the corridor, Jimmy could hear a piano playing. It was coming from one of the classrooms near reception. He wondered if he could sneak by and take a quick look. There wasn't anybody around so, sneaking past reception, Jimmy headed towards the music.

The door of the classroom was like the ones at Penham High – having a pane of glass you could peer through from outside. There was a small group of pupils – about year nine Jimmy guessed – standing around a piano at which sat a teacher with bright red hair. Red as in scarlet and the most shocking shade Jimmy had ever seen and he'd certainly never seen it on a teacher before. How cool was that? He wondered if all the teachers in the school were as wacky.

But singing? He hadn't known drama schools did that. Did all the pupils sing? Jimmy's music teacher at school was always telling him that he had a great voice and that he should join the choir, but he'd been put off by the thought of Stoner and Wicks and his classmates. It was bad enough being a would-be actor without having the label of 'choir boy' attached to him as well. But, at drama school, that wouldn't matter because it was perfectly normal and he rather liked the idea of singing. Perhaps he could even start auditioning for some of the West End musicals.

He watched the pupils for a few more minutes. He wasn't sure what the song was, but it sounded fun and Jimmy half-wished he could sneak into the classroom and join in, but he had a mission and it didn't involve singing songs so he made his way back to reception.

He knocked on the door and was immediately invited to enter. It was a tiny office with two women sitting at separate desks. Their in trays were enormous and overflowed with paperwork and the telephone was constantly ringing even though it was the end of the day.

'Can I help you?' a middle-aged lady looked up from her cup of coffee, fixing Jimmy with beady eyes from above a pair of glasses.

'I've come to apply for a place,' Jimmy said, trying desperately to sound confident.

'A place for what?' the lady asked.

'At the school. As a pupil,' Jimmy said, thinking it quite unnecessary. What did she think he was there for – the post of caretaker?

'Oh, well, you're too late. Admissions for September are over.'

Jimmy frowned, thinking he must have heard her wrong. 'But I've only just been given this,' he said, handing over his application form which he'd sweated over the night before, writing it all out first in an A4 pad before painstakingly copying it onto the form, terrified of making a mistake.

'All the places are full,' the lady said most unhelpfully, handing his form back.

'But-' he began. What was he going to say? He wanted to say something like, 'You must be wrong' or 'You don't understand' or even 'Don't you know who I am?' But he wasn't bold enough.

'Perhaps you could try for next year,' the lady said, but she might as well have said, 'Why not become an astronaut' because next year seemed like a million miles away.

He left the office with his application form, passed the classroom where the voices were still singing loudly and cheerfully as if to mock Jimmy. *'You don't fit in here,'* they seemed to say. *'What made you think you could get a place here?'*

He walked along the corridor of happy photographs and a tiny part of him wanted to tear them down from the walls.

Why? Why had he thought he could just walk into a drama school? What had made him believe that?

Ben Farley.

'Ben!' Jimmy almost shouted the name. The reference! He'd forgotten to give them the reference.

He did an about turn and headed back to the office, knocking on the door and entering again, but the lady receptionist was standing up ready to leave for the day.

'Did you forget something?' she asked, frowning at his return.

'Yes,' Jimmy said. 'I've got a reference,' he said, proudly handing over the prized document. 'From Ben Farley.'

'Ben Farley the director?' she asked.

'Yes,' Jimmy said with a smile. 'And here's my application form,' he added, handing it over for the second time.

'It's still late,' the lady said.

'I know,' Jimmy said. He just knew he had to give it a go. He couldn't leave without having at least tried.

The lady opened the envelope and took out the reference, her eyes glancing at the same glowing words that Jimmy had read and reread on the tube. Would it make a difference?

'I'll pass it on for you,' the lady said.

'Please,' Jimmy said, feeling much more confident than he had a few minutes ago.

He was just leaving when the other lady from reception followed him out.

'Young man!' she called. Jimmy turned. 'I thought you might like to look at this.' She handed him a prospectus of the school. 'It's got all the information you'll need to know if we call you for an audition,' she said, smiling. 'Good luck!'

Jimmy took it and thanked her.

Heading back down the corridor, the singing now seemed to cheer him on, and the pupils in the photographs seemed to smile down at him, daring him to join them.

'I will,' Jimmy said. 'With a little bit of luck.'

15. FISH PIE AND CONFRONTATIONS

Rehearsals continued and the cast of *Family Matters* graduated from the studio at the back of the Countess Theatre to the stage itself. That's when the really hard work began. Everybody had learned their lines by then, but they had to rethink their body language and movements in order to make the best use of the space. Then there was voice projection. It was a large theatre and the people in the back row of the upper circle would be expecting to hear you just as clearly as those paying top prices for the front row, but this didn't mean bellowing your lines.

Jimmy was having a ball. The days passed by in a blur of bliss. He completely forgot about his application to *The West London Stage School* and immersed himself in his role as Philip Tranter.

Then, finally, they were doing dress rehearsals and Jimmy found himself sharing a tiny room at the back of the theatre with Chris and experiencing the strangeness of make-up.

'Why do we have to wear this?' Chris complained as his face was smeared with foundation.

'The lights in the theatre will bleach you white and make you look horribly shiny if you don't wear it,' the young make-up girl explained.

'But eye-liner,' Chris complained. 'Do I have to?'

'Stay still or I'll poke your eye out,' the girl said.

Jimmy stifled a giggle and watched, knowing it would be his turn next.

The stage was now set as the Tranter's living room and, when Jimmy first stepped into it, he felt that he was truly entering a different world. There was the dining table where he and Chris would have many a heated discussion, the sofa where Jimmy would share a tearful scene with his stage-mother, and the front door which would reveal the surprise ending.

The costumes had all arrived too and had been fitted to perfection and given several trial runs in dress rehearsals, and the programmes had been printed with Jimmy's name which was the best feeling in the world.

'Looks like we've made it,' Chris said as he flipped through his copy of the programme.

Jimmy nodded. He'd never felt so excited in all his life. Everything was set for opening night.

All he had to do now was tell his mum.

'It makes a nice change to have you home early,' Jimmy's mum said as she untied her apron and laid the table for dinner. 'How's Chris?'

'He's fine,' Jimmy said.

'And all this maths cramming after school together seems to be helping?'

'Oh, yes,' Jimmy said. He'd told his mum that's why he was always late home each evening and his mum had believed him. But he was going to have to tell her what was going on – and soon. Opening night was in a week's time. 'Anyway,' he continued, 'I wouldn't want to miss dinner.'

It was a cooking night in the Catesby household and his mum's elbows and cheeks were dusted with flour and every utensil in the kitchen had been used and chucked into the sink. Jimmy watched as she poured them drinks. She was in a good mood and he wondered – just wondered – if now would be a good time to tell her about his impending role in *Family Matters*.

'Mum?'

'Hmmmm?' she said, bending to open the oven door. 'Oh, my good lord.'

Jimmy bit his lip as he waited to see what was about to emerge. It was meant to be some sort of fish pie, but something had gone horribly wrong and the dish that his mum extracted from the depths of the oven seemed to be filled with boiling frogspawn.

She placed it on the mat in the centre of the table and Jimmy stared at it in undisguised horror. Perhaps now wasn't such a good time to tell her what he'd been up to in London.

'I don't know why I bother,' she said, her voice cracking as if she were about to cry.

'It looks lovely,' Jimmy said, quickly replacing his look of horror with one of joy.

'Well, maybe it will taste all right.' She picked up the serving spoon and dollopped a serving on each of their plates. Jimmy watched as it slid and splurged until it finally came to rest in a white lumpy lake. 'It did NOT look like this in the recipe book.'

'But those photos are all fake aren't they? They probably reinforced it with superglue,' Jimmy pointed out.

His mum tried to smile, but her eyes looked watery.

'I wish-' she started to say, but was interrupted by the phone.

Jimmy poked the fast-cooling food with his fork and dared to take a tiny mouthful as his mum went to answer the phone. It really wasn't that bad. If only it didn't look like dog vomit.

'What? I don't understand you,' his mum's voice said from the hallway. 'Now, just a minute. My Jimmy's a good student. He's been working extra hard if you must know and, being his form tutor, I would've thought you'd know about his extra maths lessons.'

Jimmy gulped. It was Mrs Huddlestone.

'How long? I don't believe you. Don't use that tone of voice with me,' his mum shouted down the phone. 'Well, *I'm* trying to sort things out *too*.'

There was a moment of pained silence and then his mum came back into the kitchen.

'JAMES CATESBY!' she yelled. 'I think you've got some explaining to do.'

The fish pie was forgotten.

Jimmy explained as best as he could whilst his mum paced up and down the kitchen, her face the colour of a boiled beetroot. She didn't interrupt which, if anything, made it worse as Jimmy had the feeling she was saving all her fury up for one big explosion when he'd finished.

'I didn't think I'd get the part,' he said, 'so I didn't tell you about the audition and then I thought you'd be angry with me – especially with missing school.'

He paused.

'You've always told me the truth, Jimmy. Why didn't you tell me what you were doing? His mum's face creased into angry lines. 'So all that about maths lessons and Professor Nutberry was lies?'

Jimmy nodded dolefully.

'Who's Chris, then?'

'He's in the play. I met him at the audition.'

'And he knew that I didn't know about the play,

didn't he?' His mum's voice sounded brittle and sharp, as if she had it in mind to ring Chris and give him a piece of her mind. 'He was plotting along with you, wasn't he?'

'It's not his fault, Mum.'

'Good lord, Jimmy! Who put all this acting stuff into your head, anyway? How did you find out about this audition?'

'Miss Snow told me about it.'

'Miss Snow?'

'Mary Snow.'

'The actress?'

'She lives in Penham Manor.'

'I know that,' his mum said angrily. 'How do *you* know her?'

'I met her.'

'How?'

Jimmy swallowed. Was he also going to confess to being bullied and leaping over walls into people's gardens as well as taking parts in a West End show on the sly? He decided not to.

'I met her in the village. We got talking.'

His mum suddenly grabbed him by the arm. 'Come on,' she said.

'What are we doing?'

'We're going to visit this Miss Snow.'

'Mum, no!'

'Come *on*, Jimmy. NOW!'

His mum drove through the village like a superhero on a mission, pulling up outside Penham Manor with a screech of brakes and a vicious pull on the handbrake.

'It's very late, Mum.'

'It is rather late, isn't it, Jimmy? You should have told me *much* sooner.'

Jimmy rolled his eyes at his mum's deliberate misinterpretation of his words.

'She's old, Mum,' Jimmy pointed out, wondering if Miss Snow might actually be in bed.

'Then she should be old enough to know better than to meddle in other people's business.'

They got out of the car and Jimmy's mum marched him across the road and knocked on the door. The living room light was on and it didn't take long before Miss Snow answered the door.

'Why, Jimmy! What a nice-'

'Miss Snow?' Jimmy's mum interrupted. 'I'm Jimmy's mother and I'd like a word with you.'

Miss Snow looked a little surprised. 'You'd better come in, then,' she said, and they all trooped into the living room. 'Please, have a seat.'

'No, thank you,' Jimmy's mum said, 'I don't intend being long. I came to tell you to keep away from my son. I can't believe you'd be so irresponsible as to encourage him-'

'Just a minute,' Miss Snow interrupted. 'I don't even know your name, dear.'

Jimmy's mum looked perplexed. 'Mrs Catesby – Fiona Catesby.'

'Fiona Catesby?' Miss Snow repeated with a strange look in her eyes.

Jimmy looked from Miss Snow to his mum who was frowning. What was going on? Had they met before?

'Look,' his mum started again, 'I will *not* have my son skipping school to pursue an unpredictable vocation like acting. It's not on. You shouldn't have encouraged him.'

'Mum!'

'Be quiet, Jimmy.'

'But she's been so kind to me.'

'Jimmy! Be *quiet!*' his mum shouted and then turned to Miss Snow again, anger glowing in her eyes. 'You shouldn't have encouraged him and I'm furious that you thought you were doing right by going behind my back. I don't want you having anymore to do with my son, is that understood?'

Miss Snow looked as if she was about to say something, but Jimmy's mum grabbed him by the arm for the second time that evening. He tried to turn back to look at Miss Snow, but his mum pushed him towards the door.

'Come on, Jimmy. We're leaving,' his mum said, not even allowing Jimmy a chance to say goodbye.

16. FIONA CATESBY'S SECRET

Jimmy was sent up to his room, his tummy rumbling from having eaten only a couple of mouthfuls of his portion of fish pie. His mum hadn't spoken a single word to him on the way home from Miss Snow's. She'd driven in stony silence, staring out at the road in front of her as if Jimmy wasn't there at all and, when they'd got back home, he'd known better than to ask for something to eat.

As he was going upstairs, his mum had said, 'And you'll quit the play, Jimmy.'

He'd immediately opened his mouth to protest, but she wasn't having any of it.

'You'll quit the play. You can ring up tomorrow.'

Jimmy had wanted to scream and shout like a toddler. He'd wanted to throw the biggest tantrum of his life: to pound the walls with his fists and stamp through the floorboards with his frustrated feet. But he knew it wouldn't do any good. In his heart of hearts, he'd known this would happen. What had he expected? He'd known his mum's feelings about his acting obsession all along and yet he'd let himself believe – hope – that she'd come round.

'A play?' she might have said. *'In the West End? My Jimmy? Oh, my goodness! I can't believe it. I mean, I thought acting was just a phase you were going through. I didn't realise you had real talent. Oh, Jimmy! I'm so proud of you. I'll book a ticket for every performance. Oh, my sweet, clever boy!'*

Who was he kidding? As if that was likely to happen.

Lying on his bed, Jimmy stared into space. After the highs of the last few days, he had never felt more miserable in his life. He thought of Chris's words to him when they were looking through the theatre programme. 'We've made it,' he'd said. Well, not quite. Chris had made it, but Jimmy might as well have tried to conquer Everest.

He stared at the posters on his walls. The friendly, familiar faces of Cary Grant, James Stewart and Tom Hanks smiled down at him.

Cheer up, Jimmy, they seemed to say. *You'll make it yet.*

'How?' Jimmy asked. 'I'm too young to run away from home. I've got no money and nowhere to go. The drama schools wouldn't take a homeless person, would they?'

He remembered his application for drama school. What a wasted dream that had been too. He'd been given a glimpse of the life he so longed to lead, but it had been cruelly snatched away.

But, perhaps what was worst of all was the fact that he had to tell Ben. Ben had been so good to him – believing in him, pushing him to give the very best of performances, and was this how Jimmy was going to repay him – by pulling out at the last minute?

He closed his eyes because he couldn't see a single way out of his dilemma.

Jimmy rang Ben first thing the next morning before his mum dropped him off at school – which she was doing to make sure that he actually went.

It was much worse than he could ever have imagined.

'What do you mean, Jimmy?' Ben had yelled down the phone. 'You're our star! What's everyone going to think? What's Chris going to say?'

Jimmy hadn't even thought about what Chris might think. There were so many people he was letting down.

'I'm sorry,' he'd said, cursing the useless word, but it was all he had to offer.

Jimmy tried so hard to reason with his mum too.

'I'll be getting paid,' he told her.

'I'm the breadwinner in this household,' she said, her head tilted proudly. 'I don't need my son to work.'

'It'll be good experience – for the future,' he said.

'You'll get plenty of experience soon enough. You don't need to start now.'

He quickly moved on to trying to appeal to her guilt.

'But I'll be letting all those people down.'

'That's not my fault-'

'It is-'

'You should've thought about that before. You've always known my feelings about acting.'

Then she'd taken him to school where he'd had to face Mrs Huddlestone's furious glare and the prospect of two weeks' break time detentions. It was the grimmest day of his life.

That evening, after tea, Jimmy was just finishing his French homework when there was a knock on the front door. Jimmy crept out of his room and peered over the banisters.

It was Sophia Snow.

'Hi,' she said, giving a brief smile to Jimmy's mum who scowled back at her in response.

'Yes?'

'I'm Sophia. I'm a friend of Jimmy's.'

'Oh?' his mum said as if not believing her.

'I've got something for Jimmy.'

'Really' his mum said, making Jimmy think she was going to make a scene, but she obviously thought better of it. 'You'd better come in. JIMMY!' his mum bellowed, making Sophia jump. 'You've got a visitor.'

Jimmy went downstairs and smiled at Sophia. 'Hello.'

'Hello,' she said.

For one awful moment, he thought his mum was going to make them all sit in the living room together, but she turned to Jimmy and said, 'I suppose you'd better go up to your room. It's tidy, isn't it?'

'Yes, Mum,' Jimmy said with an inward groan before trooping upstairs with Sophia behind him. What on earth was she doing there, Jimmy wondered? He hadn't even realised she knew where he lived. There was only one explanation: Miss Snow must have told her. Miss Snow must have sent her.

'You know why I'm here, don't you,' she said once they were in the privacy of his room. It was rather like a line from one of Jimmy's film noir movies.

'Miss Snow sent you?'

Sophia nodded conspiratorially. 'She knew it would be difficult to speak to you and she's got something she thought might interest you.' Sophia handed him an envelope.

'What's this?'

Sophia shrugged. 'I guess you'd better read it.'

Jimmy tore the envelope open and read the neatly sloping handwriting of Miss Snow.

Dear Jimmy, I'm so very sorry if I've got you into trouble. It was the last thing I wanted to do and now I'm afraid I've lost you as a friend too.

I think you noticed my curiosity at your mother's name the other night. My memory is so bad and it bothered me all evening before I finally realised where I knew her from. I don't want to cause any further trouble, but I do think you should know.

With very best wishes from your loving friend,

Mary Snow.

Jimmy looked up from the letter completely baffled. 'What does she mean?'

Sophia shrugged again. 'Don't ask me,' she said. 'I'm just the messenger.'

'Is that all? It doesn't tell me anything. I don't understand.'

Sophia looked equally baffled for a moment. 'Oh!' she suddenly said, taking her bag from her shoulder and opening it up and brought out what looked like a scrapbook. 'She wanted you to see this.'

Jimmy took it from her and sat down on his bed with it, Sophia sitting beside him. Opening it up, he discovered that it was, indeed, a scrapbook, and it was filled with newspaper clippings. They seemed to be dated from the nineteen-nineties and featured Miss Snow.

'Why does she want me to see these?'

'I really don't know,' Sophia said. 'I'm just-'

'The messenger,' Jimmy finished for her.

'She's got hundreds of scrapbooks like this and she said this was the important one.'

'But I don't know what I'm supposed to be looking for,' Jimmy said, turning the pages and briefly reading the headlines and scanning the photographs. They were mostly of Miss Snow, of course, or about productions she'd been in. There was the production of *Hamlet* she'd mentioned to him before. There was her scary-looking Lady Bracknell. But why did she want him to see all this?

Then something arrested his attention and his mouth dropped open.

'What is it?' asked Sophia who was watching him.

Jimmy couldn't speak. He just pointed. Sophia looked down at the newspaper clipping and read.

Fiona's Fatal Flop.

'What does that mean? Who's Fiona?'

Jimmy looked up at Sophia. 'She's my mum,' he said.

Sophia's eyes widened. 'Your mum? Downstairs?'

'I've only got one mum.'

'Wow!' she said, looking at the photograph closely. 'She was really beautiful.'

Jimmy frowned. 'She still is,' he said, surprised at how quick he was to defend his mother even though she'd caused so much trouble lately.

'I didn't know she was an actress,' Sophia said.

'Neither did I,' Jimmy said. 'She's never said anything about it.'

'So what's this clipping about? Are you sure it's her?'

'Look: *Fiona Catesby in theatrical fiasco*,' Jimmy said, reading the caption under the photograph of his mother.

'What's this all about?'

'Shush!' Jimmy said, desperately reading the article. It was dated May the twelfth, nineteen ninety-five and the story began:

It was billed as 'The Best Show in Town' but, last night, The Theatre Royal closed its doors on JD Millard's production of Absent Friends. The show, which starred movie legend, Mary Snow, closed after just one week.

'It's a great shame,' Miss Snow said. 'Some plays need a little more time for the public to warm to them.'

Fiona Catesby, 23, better known as the Sunshine Shampoo girl, left the theatre in tears after audiences left in droves during the interval.

Jimmy couldn't believe what he was reading. 'She was an actress. I can't believe it. *And* she starred with Miss Snow.'

'Wow!' Sophia said. 'Why didn't she tell you?'

'I don't know,' Jimmy said.

'And you never knew she was an actress?'

'No. Never. But it must be where *I* get it from. Why didn't I think of that? I've always assumed I got my acting genes from the father I never really knew. I had no idea they'd be from my mum. She's always been dead against me being an actor.'

'And now we know why,' Sophia said.

Jimmy frowned. 'I can't believe what happened to her. Why hasn't she ever told me? It's such a big part of her past.'

'And she was in TV commercials too.'

Jimmy nodded. 'That's so weird. Do you think she gave up because of this show's failure?'

'No wonder she doesn't want you being an actor.'

'But that might not happen to me.' Jimmy was suddenly angry. 'Why would she think it would?'

Sophia sighed. 'She probably doesn't. Maybe she'd just trying to protect you.'

'But I don't want to be protected.' Jimmy closed the scrapbook and got up off the bed.

'What are you doing?' Sophia asked.

'I'm going to show her this.'

'No, Jimmy. You mustn't.'

'Why not?'

'Because it will only embarrass her. If she's never told you then it's for a reason.'

'She's lied to me.'

Sophia's forehead crinkled. 'No, she hasn't.'

'Why are you on her side?'

'I'm not on anyone's side. I'm trying to understand – that's all – and I don't think it's a good idea to show that to her,' Sophia said, pointing to the scrapbook. 'There's no telling what harm it will do.'

Jimmy shook his head. 'So what should I do?'

'Talk to her about it. Tell her how you feel.'

'How am I going to do that?'

Sophia smiled sweetly as she got up off the bed. It was, perhaps, the first time he'd seen her smile properly and it lit up the whole of her face.

'You'll be fine.' And then she leaned forward and kissed him on the cheek. Jimmy felt his face flare up in a blush.

'I'm going to go,' Sophia said, putting the scrapbook back in her bag. 'But let me know what happens, okay?'

Jimmy nodded and watched as she left without saying another word, walking back down the stairs to put her shoes on. He waited, hearing the front door open and close.

'Jimmy?' his mum called upstairs. 'Come here. I want a word with you.'

Jimmy swallowed. He wanted a word with his mum too.

17. LIKE MOTHER, LIKE SON

Jimmy's mum was standing at the living room window watching Sophia Snow walking down the road. Jimmy was watching too, noticing how her vanilla-blonde hair drifted out behind her like a comet's tail. She'd been in his room, he thought, and she'd kissed him too, and he hadn't even been friendly. It had been rather difficult under the circumstances, though. After all, it wasn't everyday that you found out your mother had been a star of stage and screen. He only hoped Sophia had understood.

'Is she a friend from school?'

Jimmy bit his lip. He might as well be honest now, he thought. There wasn't much more damage the truth could do. 'No,' he said. 'She's Miss Snow's granddaughter. She's in the play.'

Jimmy's mum frowned. 'With you?'

'No. She was in one of the other families. There were three sets of children – we were going to do two nights each,' he explained. 'Mum?'

'What?' she snapped, obviously still in a bad mood with him.

Jimmy looked at her. Was this such a good idea? He might just tip her over the edge and end up having his pocket money stopped for the rest of the month, and yet he *had* to know the truth – he had to hear it from her. This was something that couldn't wait.

'Why didn't you tell me you were an actress?'

For a few seconds, her face was a perfect blank and then her expression changed and she glared at him. '*What?*'

'An actress. Why didn't you tell me?'

'What are you talking about?'

'Don't lie to me, Mum. I *know*.' It was Jimmy's turn to sound like the angry parent.

There was panic in his mum's eyes and Jimmy wondered if she was going to try and make a run for it to avoid having to answer him. But she didn't. She stood, perfectly still, her face now completely blank again. '*What* do you know?'

Jimmy bit his lip before playing all his cards. 'I know that you were in commercials and a West End play that was closed down.'

'But that was years ago,' she said, making it sound like Jimmy had no right to explore the not-so-distant past. 'How on earth did you find out?'

'It doesn't matter.'

'It does matter and I want to know,' she said and then her eyes narrowed. 'It's that Miss Snow again, isn't it? I've told her she can't talk to you so she sent her granddaughter over instead. Is that it? She's got no right to tell you that. Who does she think she is – meddling in our lives like that?'

Jimmy sighed. 'She's not meddling, Mum. You *knew* Miss Snow – you worked with her. Why didn't you tell me before we went over there? Why did you speak to her like that the other day? You knew she recognised you, didn't you? Isn't that why we left in such a hurry? How do you think that made her feel after she's been so kind to me? I felt really bad about that. I couldn't believe what you did.'

His mum looked completely dumbstruck as if somebody had knocked her over the head with a large heavy object. Jimmy felt sure she was going to topple over at any moment.

'Sit down, Mum,' he said, quickly guiding her to the sofa and sitting next to her. Her eyes were dazed and she seemed to be staring at nothing in particular. Jimmy was worried. He'd never seen her like this before.

'Mum?'

Her mouth fell open, but no words came out. Sophia had been right, Jimmy thought. What if he'd shown her that old paper clipping? She might have fainted or thrown a fit. It would have been dreadful. But he didn't like this non-speaking mother either. He wondered what she was thinking. *Had* he gone too far? What if she never talked to him again? What if she sent him away – not to a drama school, but a horrible, cold boarding school where all the other pupils were like Stoner and Wicks and he got picked on and called names and none of the teachers liked him and …

He shook his head. He had to get a grip on himself.

'Mum?' he tried again, placing a hand on her arm.

'I've tried to forget about it. I thought I had,' she said in a little voice. 'I really thought that was all over and done with. Why did you have to find out about it?'

'Because it's still important.'

'It *isn't*. You shouldn't have brought it up, Jimmy. It was wrong of you.'

'But it's stopping me from doing what I want to do.'

His mum was silent for a moment.

'Mum? You shouldn't let your experience stop me from trying to be an actor. And I *want* to try – more than anything else in the world. Why won't you let me? Is it because of what happened to you? Tell me. I want to understand.'

His mum's eyes filled with tears. 'Jimmy!' she mouthed. 'Jimmy!'

Jimmy hugged her and discovered that he was crying too.

He wasn't sure how long they sat like that, but it seemed an age. His mum was sobbing, her body shaking up and down as if she were on some kind of wild roller coaster.

'I'm sorry,' she said at last. 'I'm sorry.'

'It's okay,' Jimmy said, but he wasn't sure if she was apologising because of making him pull out of the play or because he'd seen her cry. He'd never seen her cry before – not like this. Sure, he'd seen her shedding a tear watching Jane Austen adaptations, but all women did that, didn't they? That was normal. This was different, though.

'It's okay,' Jimmy said again.

'No,' she said. 'That's the point. It isn't. It *wasn't* okay. It was the worst experience of my life.' She leaned back and struggled to find a tissue in her pocket, dabbing her eyes and blowing her nose loudly. 'I've never forgotten that humiliation. You carry it around with you. It never goes away. They said it was the biggest flop the West End had ever known and I was ridiculed in all the papers. It was awful. The tabloids were so cruel. *Shampoo Girl Washed Up!* And *Hair Today, Gone Tomorrow!*'

There was a tiny part of Jimmy that wanted to laugh at those headlines. They were the kind of bad puns he might have been expected to come up with for an English lesson homework, but these puns weren't funny because the journalists had fired them at *his* mother.

'But it's not your fault if a play's bad,' Jimmy reasoned.

'That doesn't matter. Nobody will work with you.' His mum was sitting on the edge of the sofa now and her shoulders were slumped. She looked as if all the air had leaked out of her. 'It was my first big break, you see. I'd done a few commercials before that, but this was my first proper acting challenge and I thought it was the beginning for me but nobody would work with me after that. I became invisible. I'd been tipped for the top before that, but then my agent dropped me and the phone stopped ringing. I had to start again. Do you know what that's like? It isn't easy. Your self-esteem plummets and you begin to wonder if it's all worth it.'

'Mum-'

'No, Jimmy. You've got to listen to me. When you started going on about being an actor, it nearly broke my heart. You reminded me so much of myself when I was your age – so full of hope and dreams of the future. I knew I had to stop you.'

'But I don't want to be stopped. I want to do it. It's the only thing I *really* want to do. I wish you'd understand.'

'But I *do* understand. Don't you see? That's why I'm trying to stop you. You've got time to change. You don't have to go down the same path that I went down. It's not too late for you. Think of all the other things you could do. You're good at all sorts of things at school.'

'MUM!' Jimmy shouted. 'You're not listening to me!'

'What?' His mum's eyes were bright with fresh

tears and she blew her nose again.

'I don't mind if I'm a failure.'

'What do you mean?'

'Well, I probably would,' he said, remembering how he'd felt after Ben had shouted at him, 'but I'm willing to risk it. I can't think of anything else I want to do. I just have to give it a go. Do you understand?'

Jimmy's mum's eyes crinkled in misery. 'Oh, Jimmy. I wish I *didn't* understand.' She looked at him, biting her lip and shaking her head. 'I just don't want you getting hurt. It's the most awful feeling in the world and I never want you to know what that's like. Everyone deserts you. The friends you think you have – people in the business who said they'd always be there for you – they all give up on you. Nobody cares – not really. It's every man for himself. That's what I learned and it was far too expensive a lesson to learn.'

'It's okay, Mum. I can cope.'

'Can you?'

Jimmy nodded, but his mum shook her head.

When she spoke, her voice sounded as hard as flint. 'I don't want you to have to cope with it, Jimmy. It's too much. I *won't* let it happen to you.' And she stood up, wiping her eyes one last time before leaving the room.

The discussion, Jimmy realised, was over.

18. THE UNDERSTUDY

When school ended on Friday, Jimmy walked straight home. There was no detour through the village to Miss Snow's. He hadn't dared visit since his mum had laid down the law.

Other than his drama lesson, it had been a dreary day at school consisting of science, French, PE and maths and Jimmy had managed to show himself up in each subject. He'd dropped a test tube in science, got his horse cut in a French hairdressers, his shins kicked in a vicious game of football, and had been a nought short in each of his sums and scored a fat zero in the class maths test.

The day was made all the more dreary by the fact that Jimmy knew that the cast of *Family Matters* – the entire cast of three families, together with understudies – were going out for a meal. Jimmy, of course, wouldn't be going.

He walked home, not even making a detour to the bookshop. He was in a mopey mood where nothing could possibly cheer him up. Even watching a favourite film wouldn't be able to lift his spirits. Not that his mum would let him watch anything at the moment anyway.

He was just turning into his road when his mobile rang. Probably his mum checking up on his whereabouts. But he saw it was a number he didn't recognise and his heart plummeted. Was this some new kind of bullying technique of Stoner and Wicks's? There'd been an assembly about a spate of nasty phone calls and texts that had been going round the school and Jimmy certainly wouldn't be surprised if Stoner and Wicks had resorted to that level of bullying.

Anxiously, he answered. 'Hello?'

'Jimmy?' the voice said, but it was very hard to hear because there was so much background noise.

'Yes?'

'It's Ben Farley.'

'Ben?' Jimmy's voice flooded with relief and he immediately recognised the noise of props being shifted backstage.

'How are things? Thought I'd ring and check up on you.'

'Oh,' Jimmy said, 'things are good.'

'Yeah?'

'No,' Jimmy said quickly, feeling he could confide in Ben. 'They're about as bad as they could get without me being run over by a bus.'

He heard Ben sigh. 'I'm really sorry, Jimmy. We're all missing you, you know.'

Part of Jimmy was pleased to hear it, but another part of him didn't want to know. He thought he should be doing his best to shut that chapter of his life and move on but it wasn't easy.

'I miss you guys too.'

'We've got Nigel playing Philip now,' Ben said. 'He's got all his lines perfect. He knows what he's doing and I really can't fault him, but he hasn't got your spark, Jimmy. And that's what a play – a character – needs. That's what an audience comes to see. They want to engage with the characters. Anyone can learn lines and enter and exit when they need to, but you've got that extra something.'

There was a pause. What was Jimmy meant to say to that?

'Any chance of you coming back?'

Jimmy sighed. As much as he longed to hear those words, he knew it wasn't in his power to act upon them.

'I'm sorry, Ben. I can't.'

Ben said something under his breath that Jimmy suspected was very rude indeed. 'I want to talk to your mother, Jimmy. What do you think? Mary told me about the play they were in – the one that flopped – and we both think it's really unfair of her to let that experience affect yours.'

'I've said all that to her myself.'

'And what did she say?'

'What do you think?'

Ben muttered something else that sounded rude. 'Let me talk to her.'

'I don't know if that's a good idea.'

'Don't you want me to?'

'Of course I do. I'd do anything to get back in the play, but I can't see that she'll ever let me.'

'It's got to be worth a try, though?'

'She's not in a good mood,' Jimmy warned.

'That's okay. You forget I've worked with actors all my life. I've met them all. There isn't a single one that isn't temperamental – present company accepted, of course.'

Jimmy gave a little laugh.

'Leave it with me,' Ben said.

'Okay,' Jimmy agreed, but he didn't hold much hope.

Jimmy tried not to think about what the cast would be eating in the restaurant and how much fun they would be having as he was sitting in his room doing his French and maths homework. He tried not to think badly of Nigel the Impostor who was taking his place and eating his food. He tried not to hope he'd choke on his meal or have some debilitating – but not quite fatal – accident which would mean he couldn't play the part of Philip Tranter. But what good would that do Jimmy? He was sure his mum would watch a line of ten thousand understudies play the role of Philip before she'd allow Jimmy to step in.

Closing his school books at last, Jimmy headed downstairs to say night to his mum. Her bad mood hadn't lifted yet and meal times were limited to 'Here you are' and 'thanks', and bedtimes were restricted to 'Have you done your homework?' and 'Yes'. There was no conversation, no joking about, and no stories about Tracey's latest escapades at the office.

'I'm going to bed, Mum.'

She looked up from her magazine. 'Have you done your homework?'

'Yes.' He held her gaze for a moment and hoped that she could read his mind. She knew it wasn't too late – Jimmy could still make it for opening night. She knew that, didn't she?

Jimmy waited, hoping she'd say something.

'Mum,' Jimmy said.

'Night, Jimmy,' she said. That was all.

It was still dark when Jimmy was woken up by someone knocking on the front door. Actually, whoever it was wasn't knocking – they were thumping as if their very life depended on somebody answering it.

Jimmy got out of bed and went out onto the landing where his mum was tying her dressing gown around herself and ruffling her hands through her hair.

'Go back to bed, Jimmy,' she said.

'Who is it?'

'I've no idea, but I'll get rid of them. They've probably got the wrong house.'

Jimmy watched as his mum went downstairs, shaking her head and sighing loudly.

'Who is it?' she asked before opening the door.

'I've got to speak to Fiona. Fiona Catesby.'

Jimmy strained to hear. He thought he recognised the voice.

'It's Ben Farley.'

Jimmy blinked in surprise. What on earth was Ben doing at his house in the middle of the night?

Jimmy's mum opened the door. It was Ben all right. And he was drunk.

'I've got to talk to you,' he said, coming in before his mum had time to invite him. Jimmy stood at the top of the stairs where he knew he'd be hidden, but from where he could hear everything.

'You're roaring drunk!' his mum shouted. 'What business do you have coming here in the middle of the night?'

'Jimmy's my business,' Ben slurred. 'And I have nothing, but his best interests at heart.'

'I'm his mother. *I'm* the one who has his best interests at heart.'

There was a pause. 'Are you sure?' Ben said at last.

'What do you mean?'

'You pulled him out of the play for his own good, did you?'

'How dare you come here-'

'Or was it *your* own good, huh? You're too scared.

But he's not scared,' Ben slurred on. 'Let me tell you. Your boy's got guts! He's got the biggest guts I've seen in a lad his age.'

Jimmy snorted with amusement at the top of the stairs.

'I think you should leave,' Jimmy's mum said.

'And I think you should sit down and listen to what I've got to say.'

Jimmy's mum gasped in shock. 'How dare you talk to me like that. Who do you think you are?'

'I'm Ben Farley. The best director in town.'

'You're a vain pig who's horribly drunk.'

Jimmy grinned, wishing he could see what was going on rather than just having to make do with listening.

'Look,' Ben said. 'Jimmy's understudy's had an accident. Tonight. Silly idiot's broken his ankle falling down stairs and can't walk without crutches.'

Jimmy's heart skipped a beat. Oh, my goodness, he thought. Hadn't he wished some such awful fate on poor Nigel the Impostor? Was he that powerful? He shook his head. It was just a cruel twist of fate – a twisted ankle of fate – and he knew that it wasn't going to do him the least bit of good anyway. There'd be another understudy only too happy to step into the role.

He heard his mum sigh in exasperation. 'What's that got to do with us?'

'Come on, Fiona. You *know* what it's got to do with you. This is your chance – Jimmy's chance. It's not too late. Opening night's on Wednesday. It could still be Jimmy's opening night. Give him a chance.' Ben's voice was high and excitable as if he was a clockwork toy that had been wound up too tightly.

'Look,' Jimmy's mum began. 'I've already told you-'

'No you haven't. You got Jimmy to tell me and I think that was rotten of you – making that poor lad ring me up and tell me. Didn't you have the courage to face me?'

'What do you mean?'

'You knew I'd talk you round, didn't you? You're afraid of me.'

'Don't be ridiculous.'

'I'm not being ridiculous. I'm being honest. You knew you wouldn't have a leg to stand on if you spoke to me.'

'I'm speaking to you now, aren't I? And you're not going to change my mind so I suggest you leave.'

'I'm not leaving till you've heard me out.'

'I'll call the police.'

'You'll do no such thing.'

'Let go of me!'

Jimmy blinked. What was Ben doing? What was going on down there?

'Let me tell you something else you don't know about your son. I got a phone call today from Anna Martingale. Bet you don't know who she is.'

'Of course I don't and will you-'

'Only the headmistress of The West London Stage School.'

'What?'

'YES!' Ben said triumphantly. 'Jimmy's applied to drama school. That boy's got a dream and you're stopping him from pursuing it.'

'I-'

'And they want him to audition for a scholarship. How often does an opportunity like that come along?

Tell me you're really going to stop him, Fiona.'

'*Mrs Catesby.*'

'Tell me, Fiona.'

There was silence for a moment and Jimmy strained to hear what was happening and then he heard a strange sound. It was like an eerie whistling wind and it took him a moment to realise that it was his mum. She was crying.

'Fiona!' Ben suddenly sounded distressed.

'Go away! Leave me *alone!*'

'Come on,' he said. 'Come and sit down.'

Jimmy saw them as they passed the bottom of the stairs. Ben was leading her into the living room, an arm around her shoulder, and then he shut the door behind them.

Jimmy tutted. He couldn't hear a thing now. He stood at the top of the stairs wondering what to do. He could go downstairs, of course, and hover outside the door, but what if he got caught? He was getting cold, anyway so, reluctantly, he went back to bed, shivering under the covers and waiting for the door to open. He knew he wouldn't be able to sleep until he heard the door open.

But he was wrong.

19. BREAKFAST

When Jimmy woke up, he had a strange feeling that something wasn't quite right. He sat up in bed and blinked in the harsh light that poured through the gap in the curtains.

It was Saturday morning.

'*Ben!*' he suddenly said and it all came flooding back to him. Ben had been there the night before and he'd made Jimmy's mum cry. Then what had happened? How long had they talked for and what had they talked about?

Jimmy washed and dressed as quickly as he could and legged it downstairs. His mum was in the kitchen making scrambled eggs. She had her back to Jimmy and didn't turn around. Was she still in her bad mood? Or was she in an even worse one?

'Mum?' Jimmy asked in a whisper, wincing at the possibility of getting his head bitten off.

'Sit down, Jimmy,' she said.

Jimmy sat at the kitchen table. Was he in trouble? It hadn't been his fault that Ben had come round.

Jimmy waited for his mum to speak, but she remained silent, her back an impenetrable wall. It seemed to him that scrambled eggs had never taken so long to make. Finally, his mum turned around. Her face looked soft and rosy as if she'd slept well which would have been surprising in the circumstances, but she wasn't smiling. She simply divided the scrambled eggs onto two plates and buttered their toast before sitting down opposite him.

Jimmy looked at her across the table and then she did something truly horrible: she made them eat the whole of their breakfast in silence. Jimmy felt as if he was going to burst. What was going on? He simply had to know what had happened the night before.

'Mum,' he said as he finished his last mouthful of breakfast.

She raised her eyes from her empty plate. 'Yes?'

Jimmy frowned. 'Aren't you going to tell me?'

His mum looked a little startled for a moment.

'Last night – *Ben!* Tell me what happened!'

'No,' she said at last. 'I'm not going to tell you what was said between Ben and me although I'm sure you heard a great deal of it from the top of the stairs.'

Jimmy blushed.

'But what *happened?*'

His mum looked pensive and then bit her lip. 'We had a talk,' she said with a tiny smile. Jimmy blinked. He hadn't seen her smile for quite some time now. Was that a good sign?

'Yes,' she said, 'we had a talk – and that's all you need to know.'

'But, MUM!'

'Patience, Jimmy. What have I told you about being impatient? How am I meant to tell you that you're going to be in the play in time for opening night if you don't stop interrupting me?'

Jimmy's mouth dropped open. '*What?*'

'You're going to be in the play. If that's what you truly want,' his mum said, her expression anxious – almost shy.

'*If* that's what I want?' Jimmy said, his mind racing. 'I want it more than anything in the world.'

'I know. I know!' his mum said, her face creasing into a smile.

'MUM!' he yelled, pushing his chair back so hard

that it fell over in his rush to hug his mum.

'Careful, Jimmy. You're crushing me. I can't breathe!'

'Thank you. Thank you! *THANK* YOU!'

She hugged him back and they both laughed. 'My Jimmy!'

'I can't believe it! I'm going to be in the play.'

'Yes,' she said, 'and I should never have pulled you out. I'm sorry, Jimmy. I'm so sorry.'

'It's okay.'

'I was scared,' she said. 'I didn't want you to get hurt – that was all. I never meant to seem mean-spirited. I should have told you the truth from the beginning, but I was too afraid.'

'It's fine. I understand,' he said.

His mum looked at him with adoration in her eyes. 'Ben – he made me see what I already knew in my heart of hearts. It was wrong of me to do that to you. Can you forgive me?'

Jimmy laughed. 'You're forgiven,' he said.

His mum dried her eyes quickly and blew her nose. 'Oh, goodness! Look at me. What a state. And there's so much to do too. Ben's booked us a box.'

Jimmy's eyes widened. 'Really?'

'Mary and her daughter and Sophia and me – we're all in one of the boxes.'

Jimmy grinned. 'You and Miss Snow?'

She nodded. 'That's another thing I'm rather ashamed of. I should never have spoken to Mary like that. I remember she was so sweet and kind to me when we were working together and I'm hoping we'll all be the best of friends now.'

Jimmy shook his head in disbelief. 'I can't believe it. And you're really coming to see me?'

She frowned. 'Of course I am. What kind of mother would let her son star in a West End show and then not bother to go and see him? But I haven't a thing to wear. What do you wear to your son's opening night?'

20. OPENING NIGHT

Jimmy's mum pulled over outside Penham Manor and quickly checked her appearance in her compact.

'You look fine, Mum.'

'Are you sure?'

Jimmy nodded. His mum was wearing a new dress in a dusky rose colour and had treated herself to a trip to the hairdressers. Her hair was now swinging around her shoulders in glossy dark curls.

'Gosh, I haven't felt this nervous since *I* had an opening night,' she said and then she must have remembered that it was actually Jimmy's opening night. 'How are you?'

Jimmy breathed in deeply and let out a long sigh. 'Pretty nervous,' he said.

'Come on, then.'

They got out of the car and Jimmy's mum immediately reached into her handbag and lit a cigarette.

'MUM!' Jimmy shouted. 'Put it out. It'll make you stink of smoke.'

She took a couple of quick puffs and then stubbed it out with one of her pretty shoes. 'You're right,' she said. 'And I'm going to give up too – did I tell you?'

'Yes, Mum. About twenty times.'

'No, I mean it this time.'

Jimmy shook his head. He'd heard it all before.

They knocked on Miss Snow's door.

'Jimmy,' Catherine Snow said, opening the door and ushering them inside. 'Fiona, how lovely to meet you.'

'Hello,' Jimmy's mum said.

'Mother's just getting dressed and won't let us see what she's wearing.'

'I bet it's something special,' Jimmy's mum said.

'And what a gorgeous dress you're wearing,' Catherine said who was wearing a dress in a shimmering emerald green.

Jimmy saw Sophia in the living room and smiled. She rolled her eyes as their mums exchanged information about hairdressers, shoes and dresses.

'Nervous?' Sophia asked Jimmy. It was obviously going to be the question of the evening.

He nodded.

'You'll be fine,' she said.

'It'll be your turn on Friday.'

'Don't I know it? Ben's got the other box booked for you all then.'

Jimmy's eyes widened. 'Has he?'

'He certainly has. You wouldn't miss *my* opening night, would you?' She smiled at him and he grinned back, trying not to stare at her. He'd only ever seen her wearing jeans and t-shirts. Tonight, she was wearing a pretty silver dress and her vanilla hair was worn loose.

'Good evening, everyone,' a voice suddenly said.

A stunned silence fell upon the room as Miss Snow descended the stairs, her brilliant white hair swept up into an elegant chignon. She was wearing the softest, palest blue dress draped with a shawl, and diamond droplets fell from her ears.

'Mum,' Catherine gasped.

'Grandma – you look wonderful!'

'And you do too, my dear. And, Catherine, what a gorgeous dress.' The three generations of women embraced one another and then Miss Snow turned her attention to her other visitors.

'Mrs Catesby,' she said, approaching Jimmy's mum.

'Fiona, please,' she said in a quiet voice.

'I'm so sorry for the trouble I've caused you.'

'Please,' Jimmy's mum said, 'think nothing of it. I needed a shake up and I'm now so glad that my Jimmy met you.'

'I do hope we can be good friends,' Miss Snow said.

'So do I,' Jimmy's mum said, and the two of them embraced.

'And Jimmy,' Miss Snow said, turning to him at last. 'The star of our show.' Jimmy blushed as Miss Snow kissed him on the cheek. 'How are you feeling?'

'Pretty nervous,' he said for the third time that evening.

'That's good,' she said, giving him a wink and placing something in his hand.

Jimmy looked down and saw a beautiful gold watch.

'Miss Snow!'

'It was my husband's,' she said, 'and I'd be so happy if you would accept it.'

'But I …' he stopped. What should he say? He looked at his mum. It was such an extravagant gift and he wasn't sure if he should accept it.

'You've been a great friend to me, Jimmy.'

He looked at Miss Snow and then his mum who nodded and smiled.

And then he leaned forward and hugged Miss Snow. 'Thank you,' he said. 'Thank you so much.' She smelt of lavender and her hair was as soft as cobweb against his face and, for one dreadful moment, he thought he was going to cry.

A horn sounded from outside.

'Come on,' Miss Snow said. 'I have another surprise.'

They all trooped over to the window and there, in the middle of the road, was a beautiful old silver Rolls Royce and, stepping out of the driver's seat, was a chauffeur in top hat and tails.

'Oh, Mum,' Catherine shouted in glee.

'Is that for us?' Sophia asked, her face alight.

'It most certainly is. We want to arrive in style, don't we?'

'But I thought we were getting the train,' Jimmy's mum said with a laugh.

'In these fabulous dresses?' Miss Snow said incredulously. 'It's only the best for us tonight.'

There was plenty of room in the Rolls Royce and Jimmy found himself sitting next to Sophia.

'I think a drive through the village first?' Miss Snow suggested and Jimmy's mum and Catherine Snow giggled like a couple of teenagers.

'Oh, look! There's Isla!' Jimmy's mum said and the chauffeur obliged her with a honk of the horn.

Everybody waved and a perplexed Isla waved back.

Arriving at the theatre, they dropped Jimmy off at the stage door. He had to be there much earlier than the rest of them and Miss Snow had booked a table in a nearby restaurant. Jimmy and his mum had had an early tea, but Jimmy was sure that his mum would be able to squeeze another meal in if it was half as splendid as the car Miss Snow had hired.

He took a moment before entering the stage door. It only seemed like yesterday when he'd been standing in the queue of hopefuls at the audition. He could hardly believe that he was here now as a paid actor.

Entering the theatre, Jimmy made his way through to his dressing room and was greeted by Chris and their chaperone, Andrew.

'Welcome back, Jimmy,' Andrew said with a friendly smile.

'Hi, Andrew. It's good to be back.'

'Jimbo!' Chris shouted. 'I didn't really think you were coming.' He crossed the room and slapped Jimmy on the back.

'Neither did I,' Jimmy said, still astonished to be there at all.

'I couldn't believe it when Ben said you'd pulled out.'

'*Been* pulled out,' Jimmy corrected. 'I didn't volunteer.'

'Aw, man! That was cruel of your mum. I'm sorry I didn't call. I didn't know what was the best thing to do.'

'It's okay,' Jimmy said.

'So what on earth happened?'

Jimmy told Chris about the last few days and Chris stared at him in amazement.

'Your mum was an actress?'

'Yep!'

'So it runs in the family?'

'Looks like it.'

'I wish I could say the same,' Chris said. 'My dad was a bus driver and his dad was a park caretaker.'

Jimmy smiled and then he noticed there was a huge bouquet of flowers on their dressing table.

'Who are they for?' Jimmy asked.

'*You*, you idiot!'

Jimmy picked up the card and read it. '*Break a leg, Jimmy! With love from Miss Snow.*'

'You've got a great patron there,' Chris said.

'I know,' Jimmy said. 'I'll never be able to thank her for everything she's done.'

'Is she coming tonight?'

'You bet. She's in a box with her daughter, Sophia and my mum.'

Chris grinned. 'My brother and his mates are here too.'

'Cards too?' Jimmy said, noticing a line of good luck cards.

'We seem to be very popular,' Chris said, raising his chin and giving a smug smile.

Jimmy grinned, noticing there was one from his Miss Parnaby, his drama teacher. 'Come on,' he said, 'shouldn't we be in costume by now?'

Time passed by in a blur of activity. Costumes were donned, make-up applied and hair arranged.

'Everyone all right?' Ben asked, his head popping through the door.

Chris and Jimmy nodded.

'Looks like it'll be a full house and rumour has it that there are a number of good agents on their way.'

Chris swallowed. 'I wish you hadn't told me.'

'No need to panic. It's all standard.'

'Critics too?' Chris asked.

'You bet so give it everything you've got tonight.'

'Not too much pressure, then?' Chris said as Ben made to leave.

'Ben?' Jimmy called after him. 'Is it all right if I wear this watch?'

Ben stepped forward and looked at Jimmy's watch.

'Where did you get this little beauty from?'

'It was a gift from Miss Snow. It was her husband's.'

'Henry? Henry Snow? Blimey,' Ben said. 'I'd keep that safe if I were you.'

'What was he like?' Jimmy asked. 'She never talks about him.'

Ben shook his head. 'She adored him, but he was a bit of a gambler – almost cost her her entire fortune. I guess, other than the house, this is the only thing he didn't gamble away.'

Jimmy swallowed hard. He hadn't realised how precious it was.

'Better not wear it, though. I don't think it's the sort of watch Philip Tranter would have, do you?' Ben slipped out of the dressing room and disappeared down the hall.

'Put it in your pocket,' Andrew the chaperone suggested.

'Thanks. That's a good idea,' Jimmy said. He wanted to keep it near him and didn't fancy leaving it in the dressing room.

'I wish we could go and take a look at the audience,' Chris said.

'Me too,' Jimmy said, but Ben had strict rules about people hanging around where they weren't wanted and Jimmy and Chris had to wait in their changing rooms until it was their turn on stage.

'I've never felt so nervous in my life,' Chris confided.

Jimmy looked at him with wide eyes. 'Really?'

'Really.'

Jimmy had never thought Chris could ever be nervous about anything; he seemed completely invincible, but he was secretly glad that he wasn't the only one who was suffering an attack of nerves.

'I can't remember my first line,' Chris said.

'Relax,' Jimmy said. 'That's normal. I read that you need fear to drive a performance and it's normal to forget your lines before you go on stage.' Jimmy thumped him playfully on the arm. 'You'll be fine. It's just this waiting that gets to you. Once you're out there, you'll become the role and relax into it.'

'How come you're so calm?'

Jimmy shrugged. 'I'm not. Not really. But I feel strange at the same time. It's like nothing can touch me tonight.'

Chris squinted at him.

'Think about it,' Jimmy said. 'We've been through so much already – all the auditions, the Stoner and Wicks stuff, the endless rehearsals: technical rehearsals, dress rehearsals, and *full* dress rehearsals. I sometimes thought my head would explode. But I think we should try and enjoy tonight.'

'You're not nervous?'

Jimmy bit his lip. '*Of course* I'm nervous! But I'm not going to let that get in the way of enjoying myself. This is the best night of my life.'

They watched the hands of the clock in the dressing room slowly turn. It was seven thirty and Tim, the actor playing their father, would be about to enter stage right for the opening scene of the play. Jimmy was so excited to be acting on stage with him, but couldn't help wondering if he was nervous too. Tim was a professional, of course, but did that stop you from being nervous? Miss Snow had said that she got nervous before each and every performance.

'It's a blessing in disguise,' she'd told Jimmy. He

really wished that she was here for a moment, just to reassure him. Surely there was no more lonely profession than acting, he thought. You were truly alone – living inside your own head. Nobody could get in there with you and help you out if you stumbled. There was the prompt, of course, but Jimmy hoped with all his heart that he wouldn't need his help.

The clock ticked round. Jimmy and Chris weren't due on stage for the first fifteen minutes and a tannoy system allowed them to hear what was going on out on the stage.

Then, suddenly, it was time and the two of them left the safety of the dressing room and made their way to the stage, waiting in the wings for their cue. Jimmy's heart was hammering. He put his hand in his pocket and felt the gold watch, his thumb stroking the cool strap.

'Okay?' Ben was behind them.

They nodded, both completely speechless.

'It's a great audience,' Ben said. 'Show them what you can do, lads. You're the best.'

And then they were on. Jimmy wasn't really aware of very much after that. He was Philip Tranter. He didn't notice the rows of faces staring up at him from the stalls or those staring down from the dress circle and upper circle. Nor did he get the opportunity to look for his mum or Miss Snow and Sophia in the box.

When he left the stage after his first scene, Grace, his stage mother, hugged him in a warm embrace.

'That was brilliant, Jimmy.'

He stared at her. 'It was?' He couldn't remember a single thing. He could only feel his heart pumping wildly.

There was a mad rush of a costume change and Jimmy was careful to take the watch out of one pocket and place it in the pocket of his new costume so that it would stay with him.

Scene after scene followed. It was sheer magic. There was a kind of electricity buzzing around the theatre that night that Jimmy hadn't experienced before. He believed it was coming straight off the audience. That's what had been missing up until now. They'd all done their part learning their lines and making the performances their own, but it meant nothing without an audience. And they were responding too. Jimmy heard them laughing at the ridiculous scene with Tim and Grace and the Yorkshire pudding and the applause before the interval was phenomenal. It was the best feeling in the world.

But it was the last scene in the play that took Jimmy's breath away. He'd rehearsed it dozens of times before but the build up to the climax was quite extraordinary and, when the curtain came down, he felt quite dazed. Was that it? Was he Jimmy again? He couldn't quite tell until Grace and Chris grabbed his hands and led him forward for the curtain call.

The waves of applause rolled over him and his mouth stretched into the biggest smile he'd ever known. He looked up to the box where his mum was. She was standing up, her hands clapping wildly, tears streaming down her face. Catherine and Sophia were standing too – both smiling down at him like beautiful angels. But Miss Snow remained seated. Jimmy smiled at her. He had to remember her age. Sometimes he forgot. She seemed so young in spirit and so much like him that he often forgot she was an old lady in her eighties.

'Miss Snow?' he mouthed her name as he looked at her more closely. She wasn't so much sitting as slumped in her seat. Her daughter's hand was resting on her shoulder, but her eyes were closed. Was she asleep? Had she taken one of her little naps?

The curtain came down and Chris grabbed Jimmy, crushing him in a mammoth hug.

'We DID it!' he yelled. 'We made it! Did you hear that applause? *Did* you?'

Jimmy nodded dumbly. It was still ringing in his ears.

'I'm sure I saw Ralph Fiennes in the stalls,' Chris said.

'You didn't!'

'I'm *positive* it was him.'

'Wow!' Jimmy said. After having watched so many of his films, the thought of Ralph Fiennes watching him perform was very strange indeed.

They made a slow progress to their dressing rooms. Stage hands slapped their backs and cheered them on, but Jimmy was looking for Ben. Where was he?

'That was awesome,' Chris was saying. 'I've never experienced anything like that before – have you?'

'No, never.'

'You okay?'

Jimmy nodded. He reached in the pocket for the watch and pulled it out. Still there. For one horrible moment, he thought it might have fallen out onto the stage and been lost.

'Where's Ben?'

'I don't know,' Chris said.

They were back in their dressing room and Jimmy sat down, his head spinning. What happened now? He hadn't been in this situation before. He glanced at Chris who looked completely stunned, as if his brain had left the building.

'JIMMY?'

Jimmy turned round. Someone was calling him.

'Ben?'

'JIMMY! Where's Jimmy?'

'I think he's in his dressing room,' someone said from further down the hallway.

Jimmy got up and went to the door and was greeted by a harassed-looking Ben.

'What is it?' Jimmy asked, concern in his voice.

Ben swallowed. 'It's Miss Snow,' he said, and the sound of applause finally stopped ringing in Jimmy's ears.

21. CURTAIN CALL

Jimmy was ushered out of the stage door where his mum was waiting for him, a taxi pulled up by the pavement.

'What's happened, Mum?'

'I don't know,' his mum said. She was crying. 'Mary fell unconscious in the theatre. Catherine phoned for an ambulance and they've all gone to the hospital.'

They got into the taxi.

'Sophia too?'

His mum nodded as the taxi sped out into the traffic.

Jimmy held his mum's hand as she stared straight ahead. He felt completely numb.

'Jimmy?'

He looked at his mum. 'Yes?'

'I just want you to know you were wonderful tonight. I'm so proud of you.' She rested her head on his shoulder and they were silent for the rest of the ride to the hospital.

'Where is she? Why can't I see her?' Catherine Snow was demanding of a young nurse when Jimmy and his mum arrived.

'She's in safe hands,' the nurse assured her. 'The best thing you can do is to wait here.'

'Catherine!' Jimmy's mum called.

'Oh, Fiona! Thank you so much for coming.'

They ran towards each other and hugged tightly as if they were old friends.

'Any news?' Jimmy's mum asked.

Catherine shook her head. 'Nobody will tell me anything.'

'I'm sure she's getting the best possible care. Come and sit down,' Jimmy's mum said.

Catherine Snow and Jimmy's mum took a seat and Jimmy walked over to where Sophia was sitting; she looked strangely out of place in her long silver dress.

'You okay?' Jimmy asked, sitting on a chair beside her.

Sophia nodded, but Jimmy could tell she'd been crying.

They didn't speak for a few minutes. Jimmy didn't think it was right to ask her all the questions he had and waited for her to speak first.

'She looked so pale, Jimmy. I've never seen her so pale.'

Jimmy remembered how pale Miss Snow had looked when he'd seen her in her bed the day after Stoner and Wicks's prank. He'd felt completely helpless and yet he'd so wanted to help. Maybe, if he saw her now, he'd be able. He must be able do *some*thing even if it was just holding her hand.

'I wish I could see her,' he said.

Sophia sighed. 'Me too. I don't know what they're doing. It's so awful having to wait.'

'What exactly happened?'

'We don't know. One minute she was watching the play and then she said she was very tired. I thought she was having a sleep, but we couldn't wake her up, and she felt so cold.'

Jimmy reached out and placed a hand on hers. She looked up at him and gave a tiny smile.

'I feel so sorry that this has happened on your special night,' she said in a small voice.

'Don't feel sorry about that. It doesn't matter.'

'But you were so good. I really enjoyed the play. It's rather odd watching it as a member of the audience. I'd never really seen it before. I don't suppose you can when you're in it.'

Jimmy smiled. 'I'm glad you liked it.'

'And you'll get a chance to see it on Friday, won't you?'

'I hope so.'

'Of course you will. And Grandma will be there with you, won't she?'

Jimmy bit his lip and then nodded, hoping with all his heart that she would be. But what if she wasn't? It was too awful to think about. He'd known her for such a short time and yet couldn't imagine his world without Miss Snow in it. She was one of life's wonderful people – full of warmth and love – and he couldn't bear the thought of losing her.

They sat silently for a few moments. Jimmy wracked his brain for something to talk about, but no subject came to mind. Hospitals weren't particularly conducive to lively conversation.

'Can I get you a coffee or something?' he offered, remembering people going back and forth to coffee machines in films set in hospitals.

Sophia shook her head.

It was a stupid thing to offer. He took out the watch that Miss Snow had given him and put it on properly. It was beautiful. He looked at the time. It was nearly eleven o'clock. He hadn't realised it was so late and yet it had only been a few short hours ago when they'd all been together in the Rolls Royce having such a good time. Who would have thought that the evening would end at a hospital?

'Ms Snow?'

Everybody looked up as a doctor approached.

'Yes?' Catherine's face was drawn and expectant.

'I'm so sorry. We did all we could to revive her, but she didn't regain consciousness. She slipped away a few minutes ago.'

'Mum!' Sophia leapt to her feet and ran into her mother's arms.

Jimmy watched in stunned silence. It wasn't possible. Not tonight. Tonight was their special night. She couldn't die tonight!

Getting up from his seat, Jimmy ran towards the toilets. He suddenly felt very sick.

'*Jimmy!*' his mum called after him.

It was only when he was stood in front of a mirror above the sinks that he realised his face was a mess of stage make-up and tears.

The funeral was the biggest that Penham had ever seen. Actors from stage and screen filled the church pews and a loud speaker system had been set up to allow those who crowded the churchyard to be able to hear the service.

The world's press seemed to be in attendance too and a number of policemen were on duty to keep traffic and people moving through the village.

Jimmy and his mum sat together in the front pew. Catherine and Sophia had wanted them close by.

'You're like family,' Catherine had said when Jimmy's mum had looked at her anxiously.

Ben was there too, accompanied by Chris, both wearing sombre suits and sad expressions.

Jimmy had never been to a funeral before. His grandfather had died before he was born and he'd only been four when his grandmother had died and his mother hadn't thought it appropriate for him to attend the funeral.

It was a strange experience being sat there at the front of the church. In a way, he felt that he shouldn't have been there at all. He felt kind of fake. He'd only known Miss Snow for a few short months. He was probably her newest friend there, and yet he'd felt so close to her. It had been a curious friendship. She'd been eighty-six years old whilst he was only twelve. That was seventy-four years difference between them. But that hadn't mattered. In fact, neither of them had ever mentioned their ages. What did it matter how old a person was?

Jimmy had never really known an elderly person before. There was old Mr Chapman across the road, but he walked around in his own grumpy world, barely acknowledging the existence of anyone else. Miss Snow had been different. She'd been an equal – a true friend.

And now she was gone.

Jimmy felt tears sting his eyes, but blinked them away. He had to be strong for Sophia who was sitting so still and silent next to him. How must she be feeling, he wondered? Miss Snow had been her grandmother and they'd obviously been close. He wondered if he should reach out and hold her hand, but he didn't want to upset her even more. In all the films he'd seen, as soon as the hero offered sympathy to the heroine, she would crumble and collapse into tears. Jimmy didn't want that to happen.

The actor and director, Sir Kenneth Branagh, gave a moving reading and, after a hymn, Ben got up and addressed the congregation, telling them, quite unnecessarily, what a warm and wonderful lady Mary Snow had been.

'She was passionate about the theatre and about her fellow actors, encouraging the young to follow their dreams and beat the odds.'

Jimmy swallowed hard at Ben's words.

'And she was a staunch supporter of independent film. I'll never forget her endless enthusiasm for my projects even when everybody else had closed their doors.' Ben stopped for a moment and Jimmy became aware that he too had lost a great friend. Everybody in the church, he thought, would miss her. He hadn't really thought about that before. He turned his glance sideways for a moment and observed the rows and rows of mourners. Miss Snow's friends.

Jimmy remembered the first time he'd met her in the garden of Penham Manor. She'd been so kind and welcoming. He could have been anybody, but she'd welcomed him into her home and made him her friend.

He sat stone still, his eyes fixed on the flowers on Miss Snow's coffin. There were lilies in white and pink, yellow roses and red carnations. It was a rainbow riot of colour which she would have loved. He shook his head at the ridiculous thought. The flowers wouldn't be there if she hadn't died so how would she have been able to love them?

When the service ended, there was a slow progress out of the church with Catherine and Sophia leading the way. Outside there were flowers everywhere. People had placed them by the front of the church and along the wall of the churchyard. Jimmy's gaze caught some of the messages.

'We'll miss you so much, Mary.'

'Rest in peace, dear friend.'

'I only knew you through your films, but always thought of you as a friend.'

Had she known how much people had loved her, Jimmy wondered, as his mum linked her arm through his? Was Miss Snow looking down on them now, reading their words and listening to their thoughts? Was she there?

Jimmy shivered. It was only early June but, as they walked through the churchyard, he was sure the cool air carried the scent of lavender.

22. SUMMER HOLIDAYS

'It doesn't seem two whole months ago, does it?' Sophia said to Jimmy.

They were in the garden at Penham Manor and the August sunshine had turned it into a paradise of flowers.

'I miss her so much,' Jimmy said and then wondered if he had any right to say that. It wasn't like he'd been related to her, but his confession made Sophia smile.

'She adored you,' she told him. 'She was always going on about you. *Jimmy said this* or *Jimmy did that.* I was beginning to get jealous.'

Jimmy blushed as they walked to the edge of the pond and peered into the dark depths where the goldfish were swimming. It was the spot he had first met Miss Snow. He remembered her glowing white hair and her kind face with the sparkling grey eyes.

'Mum can't bear to sell the house,' Sophia said, looking across into the room where Catherine and Fiona were sitting. They'd become the best of friends and the four of them were spending more and more time together.

'It's a lovely house,' Jimmy said.

'It's not that mum was brought up here or anything, but it just seems so much a part of Grandma.'

'I know what you mean. She loved it, didn't she?'

Sophia nodded. 'I remember when I first saw it. It looked so huge and I thought it was far too big for Grandma and I insisted that I should live in it with her. It seems strange that we're going to be living in it now. I hope she doesn't mind.'

'I think it would be exactly what she wanted.'

They were quiet for a few moments. Sophia sat down on a stone bench near the pond whilst Jimmy trailed a long piece of grass across the surface of the dark water.

'How did you meet Grandma?' Sophia suddenly asked.

Jimmy looked up and wondered if he could confide in her. He hadn't even told his mum about the incident. But he and Sophia had become good friends. She'd been round to his house and they'd watched countless films together including several staring Miss Snow which Sophia had in her collection, and she'd helped him with his audition pieces for The West London Stage School.

Jimmy cleared his throat. 'I kind of landed in her garden,' he began. 'From that wall over there.'

Sophia frowned. 'What on earth were you doing?'

Jimmy paused before answering. He hadn't thought about that day for ages. It was one of the moments in his life that he'd sooner forget – except for the fact that that was how he'd met Miss Snow. But he felt like a different person now too. He couldn't imagine being that scared boy anymore. The old Jimmy seemed a lifetime ago. He'd changed so much since then – grown up, perhaps.

'I was running away from Stoner and Wicks – two year tens from my old school.'

'What – they were chasing you?'

Jimmy nodded. 'With the intention of catching me and beating me up.'

Sophia looked surprised. 'I can't imagine you being bullied. You seem so-'

He bit his lip. 'What?'

'*Confident!*'

'Really?' he said. 'I don't always feel confident.'

'But you're an actor – you can pretend to be confident even when you're not. That's what I do.'

He grinned. Now, why hadn't he thought of that before?

'You sounded just like Miss Snow when you said that.'

'Oh, not you as well. Mum's always saying that to me.'

Jimmy thought that Miss Snow was very much alive in Sophia. Maybe that was why he liked being around her so much. Or was it something else? He hadn't quite made up his mind yet, but he was quite sure he would be seeing a lot of Sophia in the future what with them both going to The West London Stage School. He'd been thrilled when he'd found out that she was already at the school and he'd never forget the day that he'd discovered he was going to go there himself. The official letter of acceptance had arrived a few weeks before. One of only two year eight places available had been given to him – on a scholarship too. He couldn't believe it. He'd never forget the day he'd been called to audition there.

He'd been interviewed by the headmistress, the head of year eight and the teacher with the incredible red hair. Then he'd auditioned *three* times, and was asked to sing *and* taught some dance steps to perform. It had been a very long, but absolutely fantastic day.

'I wish Miss Snow knew I'd got into drama school.'

Sophia twiddled a daisy she'd picked, watching the colours dance. 'I'm sure she knows,' she said. 'I still feel as if she's here. I guess most people would think it spooky that she's only next door.' Sophia nodded to the church. 'But I like it.'

'And I wish she knew the play's been a success. A sell out right until closing night.'

'But she does,' Sophia said. 'She saw it. I'll never forget what she said in the interval.'

Jimmy was all ears. 'What?'

'She said,' Sophia paused, knowing Jimmy was waiting in anticipation, 'she said your star will rise and rise.'

Jimmy smiled. 'But it's so sad that she didn't get to see *your* opening night.'

Sophia shrugged. 'That's okay. She's seen me in lots of other things. I was in *Mary Poppins* last year.'

'Were you?' Jimmy said in awe, sitting on the bench next to her.

Sophia nodded. 'And *Chitty Chitty Bang Bang* the year before that. You should definitely get the school's agency to put you up for musical auditions.'

Jimmy laughed. 'I think I've got a way to go before I can sing and dance as *well* as act.'

'How's Chris getting on? I hear he was up for an audition recently.'

'He got it,' Jimmy said with glee. 'It's a new ITV drama – shooting in the autumn. He's even getting his own flat in Camden.' Jimmy smiled. 'It's in the same street as the restaurant he used to work in. I think he likes walking past knowing he doesn't actually having to go in there anymore.'

Sophia laughed. 'And you've got *your* film to look forward to.'

Jimmy shook his head. 'I still can't believe it.'

'You will – when you have to get up at five every

morning for three months. Ben never lets his actors slack, I hear.'

'I know all about that.'

For a moment, Jimmy thought about the speed at which things had happened. For years, he'd dreamt of acting in plays and films, but he hadn't really known how to go about it. But, since meeting Miss Snow, everything had happened so quickly: the play, drama school and, most recently, his first offer of a role in a film. He had an awful lot to thank her for. He just hoped she knew how very grateful he was.

A voice suddenly broke into their world.

'Do you two want any tea or are you going to sit out there gossiping all evening?' It was Catherine Snow calling from the patio door.

Sophia rolled her eyes. 'Coming, Mum!' And she skipped across the lawn, her bare feet dancing over the cool grass.

Jimmy gazed across at the churchyard. Sophia was right. Miss Snow was still here, wasn't she? And, right there and then, he knew that she would live on through him and Sophia: her spirit of adventure, her passion for acting and her determination for them to succeed.

'Are you coming, Jimmy?' Sophia called as she stopped and waited for him.

'I'm on my way,' he said.

Sophia smiled at him as they walked across the lawn and went inside for tea. 'You're going to love drama school,' she said.

Jimmy smiled back. 'I know.'

ABOUT THE AUTHOR

Victoria Connelly was brought up in Norfolk and studied English literature at Worcester University before becoming a teacher. After getting married in a medieval castle in the Yorkshire Dales and living in London for eleven years, she moved to rural Suffolk where she lives with her artist husband and family of rescued animals.

Her first novel, *Flights of Angels*, was published in Germany and made into a film. Victoria and her husband flew out to Berlin to see it being filmed and got to be extras in it. Several of her novels have been Kindle bestsellers.

The Audacious Auditions of Jimmy Catesby is her second children's novel – the first, *Secret Pyramid,* is out now.

NEVER TRUST YOUR MUMMY

VICTORIA CONNELLY

Made in the USA
Charleston, SC
29 May 2015